Circle of Sinners

Lawrence Block & Hal Dresner

writing as Don Holliday

CIRCLE OF SINNERS

LAWRENCE BLOCK & HAL DRESNER writing as DON HOLLIDAY

Cover and Interior Design by QA Productions

A LAWRENCE BLOCK PRODUCTION

Classic Erotica

---

21 Gay Street
Candy
Gigolo Johnny Wells
April North
Carla
A Strange Kind of Love
Campus Tramp
Community of Women
Born to be Bad
College for Sinners
Of Shame and Joy
A Woman Must Love
The Adulterers
Kept
The Twisted Ones
High School Sex Club
I Sell Love
69 Barrow Street
Four Lives at the Crossroads
Circle of Sinners
A Girl Called Honey
Sin Hellcat
So Willing

Classic Erotica #20

Circle of Sinners

Lawrence Block

&

Hal Dresner

Chapter 1

His name was Miles Carter. He was thirty-four years old. He had brown hair that was almost black and he wore it in a shaggy crew-cut that kept him looking like a superannuated Ivy Leaguer. He was an inch or two short of the six-foot mark, with long legs and just a little too much padding in the gut. He had a high forehead and a long nose and a mouth that hadn't smiled in three weeks.

Three weeks ago, his wife had left him. His wife was—or had been, it was hard to tell because he hadn't picked up his mail and didn't know whether the divorce had gone through yet—at any rate, his wife was a dark-roots bottle blonde with her interests limited to the clothes on her back and the mattress beneath it. When he first met her, five or six years ago, he had recognized her for exactly what she was.

She was a tramp.

Obviously.

He married her anyway. You can marry a tramp knowing full well that she's a tramp, just as you can get hooked on heroin even if you are equipped with prior knowledge that it's bad for you. She was a tramp, but he fell for her the way Jericho's walls fell for Joshua. He married her, and spent five or six years trying to see if he could earn as much money as she could spend. As it turned out, he couldn't.

And she was gone.

He picked up his glass and got rid of a half-inch of rye. He was in a bar in Harlem, a place called Pig Alley—after whore row in Paris—and he was the only white man in the place. Nobody seemed to mind. On one side of him two Negroes dressed in latter-day zoot suits were drinking something called a White Cadillac, which was a shot of Hennessy in a glass of milk. On the other side, two stools down, a light-skinned hooker in a tight cotton dress was watching a drink evaporate in front of her. Miles Carter pointed at his own glass and the bartender poured more rye into it.

He wasn't exactly drunk. He damn well intended to be, before he got out of the bar and went back to the hotel where he'd been staying since his wife's departure. But he wasn't exactly drunk yet, and he could afford to take his time. It was only eleven. The bar wouldn't close until four, and after that he could always find an after-hours joint. Harlem swam with them. The drinks cost a buck and a quarter per, and you were liable to get wood alcohol and go blind, but those were the breaks of the game.

Somebody fed the jukebox and played a Dinah Washington record. Carter drank off some of the rye and listened to the music. Dinah was singing blues. He decided that he approved. That was one thing about Harlem—you got to listen to gutty music, sad music. Not the crap you got on other jukeboxes in other bars.

He was becoming an expert on jukeboxes, and on bars. Especially on bars. He still went to work every morning, doing art-layout for an advertising agency; but he was late half the time and hungover all the time, and he didn't figure they would keep him around much longer.

He didn't care.

They could can him, and that would be fine with him. He had enough money to keep going for awhile. He was staying in a roach trap hotel on Upper Broadway where the bite for rent only came to fifteen a week, and his tastes weren't too exorbitant. He had a couple thou in the bank—a miracle, because it is hard to lay away money when your wife is spending more than you are earning. But he had that couple thou, and he had a Diner's Club membership which would guarantee him a certain sort of financial independence after he ran out of cash.

Eventually he'd get over the bitch. He'd straighten out, and learn to walk past the bars. Then he would get another job. So he could hardly think of himself as the greatest loser since Job. It was a minor tragedy. He'd get over it.

Eventually.

He drank more rye. One of the sharply-dressed pimps turned, noticed him, flashed bright teeth in a smile. Carter decided it was a hell of a patronizing smile.

"Man," the Negro said, "I know just what you are looking for. And I have just what you want, man."

Carter looked at him.

"You want to ball a chick, dig? You want a wild woman who knows the score. Do I read you, baby?"

Carter finished the rye, set the glass down. "If you mean am I looking for a woman," he said, "I'm not."

"No?"

"No."

"I could put you onto a chick, man, she'll drive you wild. She goes anyway you can name, man. You name, she goes. Like a bat from that hot place."

Carter didn't answer him.

"Twenty dollars, man. Cheap at double the price."

"Forget it."

"Fifteen, man. This is quality, man. You don't find this walking around on Seventh Avenue."

"Forget it."

"You can't make fifteen?"

"I'm just not interested."

The Negro stepped back, looked him up and down. "God-dam!" he said. "Why you come up to Harlem, baby? You fay cats make it uptown, you're looking to get your ashes hauled. This is Harlem, man. This is the integration capital of the world. A white cat comes up here, finds some nice little brown bitch and deseg-regates her all to hell, man. You sure you don't want to try a little integration? I know this bitch, she—"

"I just came in for a drink."

"Man, you ain't passing, are you? You ain't one of *us*?"

"Sure," Carter said. "I'm passing. I'm really a Chinaman who got sick of Mott Street. You got some shirts that need washing? I do a velly good job."

The Negro stared.

"No tickee," Carter said, "no washee."

The Negro broke up. He slapped his hand down hard on the bar top, threw back his head and roared. He picked up his White Cadillac and drank the tires off of it. He slammed the glass down on the bar, swung around to face Carter and stuck his hand out.

"Some skin, man. I *dig* you!"

Carter shook hands with him. The Negro moved his head about an inch and a half and the bartender scurried over. He spilled rye in Carter's glass and made a fresh White Cadillac for the pimp. They touched glasses and drank and the pimp paid for the drinks.

"My name's Freddie, man."

"Miles Carter."

"Miles? You blow trumpet, man?"

"That's another Miles."

"I dig you, man. You want to cut out, man, we'll make a party. There's this set a few blocks from here, man, and we cop a few bottles of juice and just sit around and groove there. Some fellowship, man. Let's make it."

Carter worked on his rye and tried to translate the pitch into a brand of English with which he was more familiar. There seemed to be a party somewhere, and you brought your own liquor and went there, and it was fun.

Well, fine.

He finished the rye and the Negro emptied the White Cadillac's gas tank. They strode out together. 125th Street looked like Times Square wearing blackface. Neon signs winked at the darkness of the night, holes in the wall sold ribs and barbequed chicken and chitterlings and crabs, bars blared with blues and atonal jazz and gutbucket house rock. A trio of round-shouldered and round-heeled tarts marched on parade at the corner. A red-eyed junkie, very bogue, was puking in the gutter.

"Man," Freddie said, "I am loose. I am swinging."

No answer seemed to be needed. Carter walked beside him. They turned north at Lenox and headed uptown. Lenox was a little more sedate, playing Broadway to 125th's Forty-second Street. They walked past a few nightclubs, a few closed haberdasheries. The cars parked at the curb were all late-model Cadillacs.

"Three blocks up," Freddie said.

"Fine."

"You swinging, Miles? You free and easy?"

"I'm swinging."

"Solid, Miles."

And he was swinging. That was the nice part of it. He was off on an adventure, not just bar-hopping, and he was cool and loose and free and easy and everything he was supposed to be. It occurred to him that Freddie might be looking for a convenient alleyway in which to clip him behind the ear with a blackjack, but he didn't believe it. He liked Freddie. Freddie was a pimp and he probably worked his women over with a razor when they misbehaved. But he liked him.

He laughed. A month ago he wouldn't have gone into Harlem on a bet, wouldn't have stepped out on 125th Street at high noon on Easter Sunday. A month ago he'd have been at home with Little Mrs. Dark Roots, feeling safe and sound and secure as a bug in a Bokhara and trying his damnedest to talk the bottle-blonde bitch into letting him take her to bed. It was strange how a little thing like domestic tragedy could change your outlook on life. Now he would go anywhere and do anything, would take it all as it came and feel no pain.

"This set we're falling to," Freddie said. "These are people in the life, man. You read that?"

"No."

"The life is hustling, Miles. Sweet men and their cows, man. The cows in their stables. They spin records, they drink, they sit around and groove. Just so you know, man."

"I get it."

"Because you don't want to come on uncool. When you don't know people, the best thing is nothing at all. You come on like remote, you dig? You look and you listen and you drink and you stay cool. You'll make it, man."

He was confident that he would. He'd always been nervous in social gatherings, always had trouble relaxing with people because he worried what they might think of him. But now he wasn't worried at all.

"We stop here," Freddie said. "Pick up some potables, like."

"What kind?"

"Wine'll do it," Freddie said. "Just some of that old Sweet Lucy, that Thunderbird stuff. Unless you are holding long bread, in which case a bottle of Scotch would be just about choice."

They went into the package store. Carter ordered a bottle of Grant's and paid for it. They left the store, walked uptown another block, then turned west. They were off the main drag now and the neighborhood showed it. Twin rows of faded brick tenements lined both sides of the street. The gutters overflowed with broken bottles and discarded newspapers and used condoms. Freddie whistled "On The Street Where You Live" and Carter chuckled.

"Man, you picked up on that one fast. I dig your sense of humor, Miles."

They went into a building halfway up the block, walked up two flights of stairs. The stairwell smelled of cooked pork and stale urine with the sick-sweet odor of old sex in the background.

There was a lot of noise coming from behind one door on the third floor. Freddie knocked at the door and somebody opened it.

The room was filled. There were about thirty people, half men and half women. Most of the men were dressed like Freddie. The women were all young and moderately attractive. They looked like chippies, Carter decided. Which figured.

"This is my man Miles," Freddie announced. "This is a very fine stud who just came to Pig Alley for a drink."

A thin man with a pencil-line mustache shook his hand. A hooker with dyed red hair winked at him. Nobody else paid too much attention. He took the bottle out of its paper bag, crumpled the bag and dropped it on the floor. He opened the bottle and handed it to Freddie. Freddie tilted it and took a long drink straight from the bottle, then passed it back. Carter swallowed an ounce or so and looked for someplace to sit down.

There wasn't much sitting room. The place was almost unfurnished—a couple of chairs, a sagging bed, a table with a record player on it.

"That's the other Miles," Freddie said. He pointed to the record player. "He moves me, man."

Carter listened. The trumpet came in over a network of chords, came in sweet and bitter at once, twisting a melody into a vital experience. He passed the bottle to Freddie, got it back and took a long drink. He stood with his eyes closed and listened to the music, tapping his foot automatically on the linoleum-covered floor.

A girl was saying, "This was a college cat, you dig? *Co-lum-bia.* He hits on me over on Saint Nicholas Ave and he's got shaking hands and eyes that keep looking away. So rabbit-scared I thought he'd turn and run away, like, so I push up against him and get him up against the wall. I got hold of him where he lives, you dig, and I'm telling him what a motherloving *ball* we'll have . . . And I'm a sonofabitch if all of a sudden there's a twenty-cent trick down the drain. You don't get rich that way, man."

A coffee-colored girl came over to him. She had kinky hair and a pug nose. Her dress was blood-red and skin-tight and she filled it completely. Evidently she wasn't wearing a bra. He could see her nipples through the dress. He tried not to look at them. He gave her the bottle and she took a drink. She grinned at him, gave the bottle back and wandered away.

A man was saying, "When those there Russians drop a bomb I hope it lands on a police station. Hope it blows all those rollers all the way to hell. This vice squad bustard, he busted one of my fly chicks, picked her up off the street and took her in and locked her up. I had to get out of bed at eight in the morning over there and bail the bitch out. And I been paying that white mother for a year now. I been laying heavy bread on that ofay. I go up to him and ask him what's happening, you know, and he just shakes his head like he's sad. 'I got a quota to make,' he tells me. 'End of the month coming up and I got a quota to make. She'll beat it when the case comes up. Don't worry, boy.' Boy! I lay a fortune on that mother and he tells me about his quota!"

He looked around for Freddie and couldn't see him. He passed the bottle to another Negro and the man took the last drink from it. Someone else handed him the jug of Thunderbird. He swigged from it. It tasted like goat urine but he had enough of a load on not to mind. He took another drink and somebody took the bottle away.

A girl was saying, "I was bogue, man. I was hung up, an hour overdue for a shot of horse and this habit of mine is a clock-watcher. I was so bogue I could taste it all the way down to my toes. And busted with no bread and nothing stashed. So I figure all I got to do is turn a fast trick and find the man, because I got to score in a hurry. I went over on Seventh Avenue and this cat hits on me like lightning. A suit and a tie and a briefcase. I figure this is money, man. We fell up to a hotel room and he puts down ten bucks. In two or three minutes it's all over and I figure I can get out and cop a shot to ease the monkey. But this trick, man, he wants to go another round. He lays down another ten and says let's go again. I tell him no, I got things to do, cause I don't want no money now. I just want that little needle. He get ugly and says I don't get out of the room unless I give him another round of loving. I try to get past him and he blocks the door and I just pick up a lamp and let him have it right across his mother loving head. Man he fell down and he did not move. He had blood in his hair, man. He lay still as death and didn't move an eye. I think I killed that mother, man, but I didn't wait to see. I just ran out and found my man and filled myself full of H in a hurry, and I don't know yet if that trick is alive or dead." A pause. "I got his wallet and watch. He had a hundred bucks in that wallet and I got twenty-five on the watch."

Carter was over by the wall. He was talking with a short, light-colored Negro about the fight coming up Saturday at the Garden. They got into a friendly argument about Louis and Dempsey and what would have happened if they had met in their prime. Carter said Louis would have won. The Negro said Dempsey would have flattened Louis in four rounds.

He drank more wine. Freddie returned from somewhere. Freddie was slapping him on the shoulder, telling him how cool he was and how much he dug him.

"Crazy," Carter heard himself say. "Next you'll want to marry my goddamn sister."

Freddie couldn't stop laughing.

He drank more wine, and then somebody gave him a cigarette and said it was marijuana. He took a few drags, and it was. His head got lighter than air and coasted up to the ceiling. A black girl kissed him and he stuck his tongue halfway down her throat. She ground her loins into his and he let one hand settle on her behind, petting her like a puppy dog. They swayed together in time to music which was playing in their own heads and he felt her breasts against his chest. They were very large and they felt warm.

He kissed her again. Her mouth tasted of wine and cigarettes and he liked the taste. She put both arms around him and hugged him hard. Her warm mouth closed around his tongue and he thought she would rip it out by the roots. He put both of his hands on her buttocks and pulled her tight against him. She was not wearing a girdle. He squeezed her meaty flesh and she made a moaning sound.

They danced, drawing back their hips and socking their loins together. He knew he was going to take her to bed and he wanted her more than the bogue hooker had wanted her fix, but there was no urgency now. He could wait forever. He was simply grooving, high on a cloud and enjoying everything around him.

He put one hand to her throat and stroked her. Her skin was

chocolate satin. She lifted her face. Her eyes were closed, her lips barely parted.

He kissed her.

She was wearing a canary yellow dress that fit her like an extra skin. She had red shoes with three-inch spike heels. Her fingernails had silver nail polish on them. She was a few inches shorter than Carter and built like an hourglass. She moved an inch or two away from him and he let his hand move from her behind and travel slowly along the side of her body. Her flesh was firm but soft. He moved his hand all the way up and a little over until he was touching her breast.

There was a Thelonious Monk record on the record player and the volume was turned up sky-high. The set had too much bass for the speakers and the box resounded every beat. The party was thinning out a little. People were leaving.

The girl said, "My name is Allie."

"Miles."

"Let's split, Miles."

They left the room and walked into the hallway and down a flight of stairs. He smelled the cooked pork and stale urine and old sex and it smelled like home to him this time. On the second floor landing she came into his arms and kissed him. He took her face between both hands and kissed her eyes and the tip of her nose. Her lips curled in a lazy smile and he kissed her again.

They walked down another flight of stairs and out to the street. The air was cold and a wind was blowing. He put his arm around her waist and she leaned against him. He heard a woman shrieking in the distance, listened to a wine bottle smashing in an airshaft. They walked past a pair of teenagers necking on a stoop, walked past a wino in a pea jacket sprawled out against the side of a building. They turned at Lenox Avenue and walked uptown two or three more blocks, then crossed Lenox and walked half a block east. They went into a building very much like the last one. The stairwell had exactly the same odor.

At the first landing they came to he grabbed her and put his hand under her skirt. She was warm and she trembled when he touched her. He wanted to take her right there at the head of the flight of stairs. She kissed him savagely, biting his lip with sharp teeth.

"Allie—"

"Miles, baby—"

They let go of each other. They were both shaking. She led him up two more flights of stairs and over to a door marked 4-D. He stood behind her while she opened the door, rubbing against her.

She got the door open and he went inside with her. The door was equipped with a police lock, a bar of cast iron set into a plate on the floor and wedged into a catch on the door. Her room was shabby but neat. There was a double bed, a nightstand, a chest of drawers. She had a private bathroom with a sink and a tub and a toilet. Everything was cheap but clean and there was a nine-by-twelve rug on the floor with only a few cigarette burns on it.

He took off his tie, put it in his jacket pocket, took off the jacket and hung it on the knob of the closet door. She came over to him and opened the buttons of his shirt very slowly and lazily. Her eyes were sleepy, half-lidded. She pulled his shirt loose from his pants and took it off. She put it on top of the dresser, then came back to him and ran her warm hands over his bare chest.

"Old Hairy Chest," she said. "Mmmmm."

She moved closer, rested her head on his shoulder. He fumbled with the zipper on the back of her dress, finally managed to get it down. She shrugged her shoulders and the dress fell to the floor. She kicked it over into a corner, then kicked her shoes after it. He grabbed for her breasts, plump and firm in her lacy black bra, and she giggled and danced away.

He unbelted his trousers, let them fall down and stepped out of them. She darted over, reached out to touch him, then jumped back. He made a grab for her and she fell into his arms and kissed the side of his neck.

He unclasped her bra and threw it on the floor. She posed for him, hands clasped behind her head, and he looked at her perfect breasts and had to catch his breath. They were very large and very perfectly formed, with hard dark red nipples at their tips. Her breasts were a shade or two lighter than the rest of her skin, as though she had worn a halter while sunbathing. She stood very still while he took her breasts in his big hands and caressed them. They were softer than velvet.

When he stepped back she pushed her panties down over her hips and got out of them. She was nude now, nude and perfect, and he thought she was the most beautiful woman he had ever seen in his life. She knelt before him and took off his undershorts, her hands gentle as a breeze.

"I like you, Miles."

"Allie—"

"I like you. Oh, I need you. So bad, Miles."

He picked her up and put her on the bed. He lay down beside her and kissed her and she pressed her whole body against him.

It was like an electric shock. He felt her breasts against his chest, her legs against his legs, her soft, warm female body pressing urgently against his hard male body. He took her breast in his hand, squeezed. He pinched her nipple and she began to tremble.

He crouched over her, kissing her brown breasts, and she moaned urgently. He put one hand upon her thighs and she thrust up to meet it.

"Now, Miles! *Now!*"

But he made her wait. He worked on her, touching, kissing, probing, and then he could not wait a moment longer . . .

She writhed on the bed, hips churning and breasts rolling, and he found her mouth with his and kissed her. Her breasts were twin pillows for his chest and her arms were bands of steel that locked him in place and would not let him move. It lasted and it endured and it went higher and higher, until at once they reached the last plateau and the world shook and shivered, and he groaned and she screamed . . .

When it was over, sleep came at once. Sleep was deep and dreamless and dark. After an hour or two he awoke. She was still sound asleep, her face buried in a pillow, her arms outstretched. He put one hand on the back of her neck and ran it all the way down to her foot. She was soft and smooth all the way.

He put his lips to the small of her back and kissed her. He rubbed her buttocks with his hand, touched her thighs, pressed his face against her buttocks. He looked at her and saw how beautiful she was. He had never seen anything more beautiful.

After a few moments she woke up. She stretched like a cat and rolled onto her side to face him. She yawned, then broke off the yawn and smiled at him.

"Hi," she said.

"Hi."

"You were loving me up in my sleep. You're a nasty old man, Miles."

"Not so old."

"But awful nasty." She giggled. "And an awful amount of *man,* too. You sleep some?"

"Uh-huh."

"I just slept like a log. Hello, Miles."

"Hello, Allie."

"You come uptown much, honey?"

"First time."

"Truth?"

He nodded.

"You married, Miles?"

"Not exactly. My wife left me. She's getting a divorce."

"*She* left *you*?"

That's right."

"Hell," Allie said. "She must be one stupid bitch, Miles. You got any kids?"

"No."

She nodded, chewing on her lip. Then she shrugged and grinned hugely. "That was nice," she said. "I'm glad you picked tonight to come uptown."

"So am I."

"You like me?"

"Very much."

"You think I'm pretty?"

She was posing for him, one hand on the top of her head, the other on her hip. It was a perfect burlesque of the standard beauty contest pose. He extended his forefinger and touched her chin. "I think you're beautiful," he said.

"Show me."

"Show you what?"

"How much you like me."

He raised his eyebrows. "Didn't I show you enough before?"

"You showed me plenty. But that was before."

He laughed and grabbed her. He kissed her and it started all over again, the excitement, the hunger, the need. He hadn't believed it would happen. Once a night had always been enough for him, but now there was no such thing as enough.

"Miles." She was holding her breasts in her hands. "Kiss me like you did before, Miles."

He kissed her breasts. He wanted to devour them completely. He kissed her again and again and he felt her getting ready.

"Miles—"

The fury was gone this time. He made love to her slowly, almost reflectively. Their bodies moved together like two tired club fighters in the tenth round. From time to time they would stop, bodies locked together, and simply lie like that.

At the end, of course, the urgency took over. At the end she was a brood mare and he took her like a stallion... and then there was nothing but silence.

When he awoke again she was gone. A yellow dawn filtered in through the window. His mouth tasted like old tennis shoes and his body ached. He blinked at the daylight, rolled over and tried to sleep again. It did not work. He got up, went to the window and lowered the shade.

The room was horribly drab by daylight. He looked around for a moment, then began to dress. His clothes were dirty. He took his wallet from his jacket pocket and glanced at its contents. All his money was there, and he hated himself for checking. He wanted to leave her something—twenty dollars, fifty dollars but he knew it would be a terrible thing to do. So he left nothing. He opened her door, fixed the police lock, closed the door. He walked down the stairs and out of the door.

Harlem was dead and gray and foul by daylight. He managed to find the corner of Lenox and 125th. He was a white man in a black world now and people were staring at him. He got onto a subway train and headed back downtown.

He got off the subway and went to his hotel. He smoked a cigarette. It was eleven o'clock and he had missed another morning of work. He decided to miss the afternoon as well.

Allie. A chocolate-colored tart who wanted him to tell her he liked her. A Harlem hooker whom he had taken into a furnished room in a stinking tenement.

He sat very still for several minutes watching the smoke trail from his cigarette to the ceiling. Then he smiled.

There was a bleached blonde ghost that would never haunt him again.

Chapter 2

"How much?" Freddie asked.

She didn't say anything. She was sitting on the couch across from him, her legs crossed. She reached down and ran a finger up the back seam of her tinted stocking.

"How much?" Freddie asked again. He looked up from his nail clipper. "Fifty?"

Allie shook her head.

"Thirty?"

Another shake, eyes closed.

"Twenty?" His voice rose.

"No, man," she said quietly.

"How much then?" he said, loudly.

"Zee-ro," Allie said.

He sprang from his chair, gripped her tightly by the arms and stood her up. "I hope you're kidding me, girl," he said, his face very close to hers. "You better hope you're just kidding me."

Allie kept her head down and studied the needle points of his gleaming black shoes.

"*Answer me!*" Freddie screamed and shook her violently.

"Nothing," she said, looking up into his raging white eyes. "Nothing. I didn't take a cent off him. I liked him."

Still gripping tightly with his left hand, Freddie's right drew back. His mouth opened.

She thought she could feel the slap before it landed. It felt cold and hard. When it landed, she knew how wrong she had been. It was more than hard. It was like a rock smashing across her mouth. The ring. She hadn't counted on the ring. She felt warm blood on her lip and then tasted it. Salty. She put her hand up and dabbed at the blood.

"You stupid black bitch," Freddie said, spitting the words.

She thought for a moment that he was going to hit her again but his hand only flapped in the air and then slapped against the side of his pants. He wheeled and walked to the other side of the room.

"You stupid bitch," he said, wheeling again. "You know how long it took me to set him up? You got any idea the sick smiles and square talk I hadda go through with that mark? You know all the hog-laughs I took from people for bringing that ofay to the party last night? And you got nothing. You liked him!"

Allie sat down again, took a handkerchief from her purse and touched at the blood on her lip. It was still coming.

"Gimme that," Freddie said, almost pouncing on her, grabbing the purse. He tore it open and began to throw things out until he came to her wallet.

"You ain't gonna find nothing there, man," she said. "There ain't nothing to find."

"Yeah?" he said, throwing the wallet down. "Well there better be something there tomorrow, you hear? There better be my forty percent of the fifty you shoulda taken last night, you understand. You just go out and find yourself another white boy and if you like him, you go find yourself another one and then another one, until you get one that ain't hung exactly to your qualifications. And you take him for twenty bucks for me or else you're in big trouble. You understand?"

She understood. It had never happened to her before but it had happened to Chlorise once and to Sara once and to Dina twice. But never again to Dina because now she was so sliced up that even her mother couldn't look at her without turning away.

"I'm talking to you," Freddie said, snapping her chin up. "You hear what I said?"

"I heard," Allie said softly. It didn't matter what she said. She knew it made no difference. She knew exactly what was coming now and nothing in the world could stop it. Chlorise had told her. Sara had told her. And she hadn't forgotten easily. She remembered it last night when she was leading that boy up to the room. She remembered it when he was turned on with all the loving he could manage.

She remembered when she had gotten up and dressed and looked at his wallet. There was more than fifty in there, which had made her laugh because he was such an innocent. A white man drinking in Harlem with his pocket full of bread. But still she hadn't taken any. Because she had liked him.

It was that simple.

And now she was sorry she hadn't because she knew what was coming.

"I think you need a little lesson," Freddie said. "I don't think you've been paying very good attention to me, girl, Your answers ain't been very sharp and I got a feeling that your mind's been wandering. Maybe you're still back there squirming with that little white boy. I think we better have a little reminder about who we are and where we are. Take off your clothes!"

She looked up at him once, not begging, not pleading, but in simple question: Do I have to? But she knew the answer to that one beforehand too.

"Now," Freddie said. He turned and walked back across the room and kept his back to her while she undressed.

She understood why. It was his way of showing her that he wasn't interested in her body. That he wasn't doing this just for a kick. That he had seen enough naked women to write a book. Two books. He was showing her that he was just doing this for discipline.

He kept his eyes on his fingernails until she was down to her bra and panties, pink against her caramel skin. Then he looked up and she stopped and stood straight, her hands at her sides, her breasts jutting like cannon shells from the tight cups.

"Everything," he said and this time he watched her.

She felt more than naked as she unsnapped her bra and let it fall to the couch on top of her other clothes. She felt dirty. And frightened. Her skin was beginning to goose bump and her hands reached down, hooked the elastic top of the panties and slipped them down as she raised her knees high and stepped out of them. Naked, she turned and laid the panties gently on top of the bra and then turned back.

He was watching her now. She knew that there wasn't a man alive who could keep his eyes off her now. If he had seen a hundred naked women, or a thousand, or even ten thousand that very morning, she knew there wasn't a power on earth that could have kept his eyes from her then. The thought calmed her for a moment and it was just like it had been for a hundred nights with a hundred different men over the past four years as his eyes crawled over her, burned into the dark red nipples, swept down and then crawled into the darkness between her legs and stayed there.

She felt safe and superior standing there dazzling him. And then she felt rigid again as she saw his hand reach into the desk drawer behind him and pull out the razor.

He grinned, a crescent of white teeth in a black mask, as he ran a finger over the flat of the blade, flicked it once so that it caught the light and burned silver fire.

"Come on over here," he said, beckoning with his left hand, holding the razor loosely with his right.

She started to take a step forward and found she was too weak from fear. She knew she was trembling; her legs felt stiff. But inside her heart was a cube of ice crashing against her ribs.

"Come on," Freddie said, crooning. "Come to daddy, naughty baby. Come and take your punishment like a good girl."

She walked to him slowly, feeling the tears coming to her eyes and the thickness to her throat.

When she was a foot away, he reached out his hand, so gently that it deceived her, and wrenched her suddenly to him. For a moment she thought she was going right into the blade of the razor but he raised that hand up and looped the other behind her back, twisting her arm.

"There now," he said, grinning, holding her in a tight embrace, her nipples just touching his chest. "There now," he said, bringing the razor forward so that the point was at the base of her throat.

The cold steel pricked and she swallowed involuntarily.

"Uh-huh," Freddie warned. "That's dangerous, that is. We're just gonna play a little game of self-control, a little game that teaches folks to listen to what they're told and don't pay no mind to what their bodies tell them. You understand that?" he asked, almost curiously, eyes widening.

She started to nod, afraid to speak.

"Don't shake your head now," he said, pushing the blade up to her Adam's apple. "You start to shake your head and you might just find yourself with your throat cut. You just blink your eyes if you understand, you hear?"

She blinked her eyes, trembling.

"Now, come on and calm down," Freddie said. "This here's not gonna be no fun for you if you're all tensed up. Just relax now and you'll play much better, I guarantee you."

But she stiffened again as he brought the blade down, tickling against her skin and over the rise of her breast.

"Now then," he said. "This is how we play this little ole game. I'm gonna hold this nasty old razor right here!" He jabbed the point into the center of her soft dark nipple and she winced with pain.

"Uh-uh," he said. "Don't cry now. Crying's against the rules." He rubbed the razor edge gently against her nipple, scraping.

The chill went through her like an icy wind. She trembled inside but did not move.

"That's better," he said, still scraping. "You see as long as you're nice and soft there, this little old knife can't hurt you one bit. But if you ever let that little cherry tip of yours get hard . . . then," he said, rubbing with more pressure, "you're gonna find it sliced right off and lying on that dirty floor. You understand?"

She blinked, feeling the warm tears in her eyes.

"Now that's simple, ain't it?" Freddie said. "Sure, it is. But oh yeah, there's one other little thing, I forgot to mention it." He grinned lewdly, releasing her arm. "Don't move now," he cautioned and his hand came down in front of her . . .

She squirmed back and felt the edge of the razor biting.

"Watch that," he said. "You just better stay very still now. Maybe it would help if you closed your eyes because this ain't gonna be too pretty to see if you make a mistake."

She listened. She closed her eyes and felt his fingers like thick worms, beginning to probe.

"Now if you don't think about this," she heard him say gently, "then you won't hardly feel nothing. And if you don't feel nothing," he continued, his finger stroking, circling, "then you can't get yourself all heated up. And if you don't get yourself all heated up," he said, his finger begin to thrust, "then those sweet little nipples won't get no notion to stand up and point, will they? No, of course they won't. See how easy a game it is?"

She kept her eyes squeezed shut, feeling dizzy and faint with fear. His touch was warm as it moved deeper. She felt the heat beginning to rise like steam, and she knew he was getting to her and she imagined that her nipples were hardening, growing, extending to meet the razor. She tried to tense and tighten against the feeling, blank her mind and forget. But his finger continued to move, probing, exploring expertly and she felt control slipping from her, being replaced by desire.

She didn't care about the razor any more. The fear was gone. She felt her heart trembling with need, her nipples growing.

She waited to feel the cold prick of the blade, wanting it now, wanting it to plunge deep within her, to be warm and quick and then to be over. Anything but this agony.

And then it was over.

She felt the point of the razor leave her and Freddie's voice said: "You can open your eyes now, honey."

She did and saw he was grinning.

"You're the best, baby, you know that? I've had gals that have just gone to pieces under that." He laughed. "In more ways than one. And I've had others that were so dumb scared they couldn't even stand. But you were just like a goddamn statue." He shook his head admiringly. "You're one cool chick, sweetness. You must have really wanted to go for that ofay last night. I don't think there's a stud in the world that could get to you if you had your mind set against it." He reached behind him and gave her an affectionate squeeze on the buttocks.

"Go put your clothes on and earn your Freddie his money, now," he said. He shook his head again. "Man, you really are one cool chick."

She didn't stop shaking until she was two blocks away. It was like going to the dentist, she thought. You were all cold nerves while you were in there under the drill but as soon as it was over, you went all to pieces.

Like going to the dentist?

Who in hell did she think she was kidding? It was a hundred times worse. That cat was a madman. No two ways about it. She had heard about him, sure. But she had never really believed it until now. Even when she had seen Dina and was told how it had happened, she didn't really believe it. It was like a joke that was too grisly to be true.

But it was true. She knew that too well now. She had come within two heartbeats of having her tips cut off and she wasn't going back for that scene again. Not this chick, man. Find yourself another black mother to play that gruesome little game. This little chickee is gonna fly far far away.

But where? And how?

She had counted the change when she was picking it up from the floor. Pennies included, she had eighty-seven cents. That would be enough to take a taxi back to the room if she walked about five more blocks before she caught one and skipped on the tip.

Oh, she could borrow a few bucks from one of the girls for dinner but after that? She would have to hustle tonight if she wanted to make breakfast tomorrow, not to mention Freddie's fare.

Not exactly in the chips. Not precisely flush.

She stopped in her thoughts and in her tracks as she passed a travel bureau. One window was full of posters of dream places. London. Paris. Rome. Places where there was no Freddie for one thing and no Harlem for another. She didn't know about Rome but black was as good as white in London and she had heard that a good-looking dark chick was a queen in Paris.

Her eyes moved from the Arch of Triumph to a grinning black native girl balancing a basket of fruit on her head. Haiti. Now there was the scene. There was a black man's island in the sun. And to here tell about it, most of the women weighed in at about two-sixty with breasts like watermelons. She would be a queen in Haiti, no doubt about it. And she wouldn't need a round-trip ticket either.

Now how much would she need to make it down to Haiti and set up in style until the native boys noticed her? Two hundred? Four? A grand? No, that was much too much. Two, two and a half should be plenty.

She thought about going in and asking the man behind the desk but he didn't look friendly. That figured. Wasn't that always the way though? Bet he wouldn't mind slipping her a ticket to paradise, but the time of day? Not unless she could prove she had some bread first. Well, black was black and white was white and never the twain shall meet. Except maybe in Haiti.

Haiti, she thought, walking on. Figure two hundred as long as we're gonna keep the dream within reach. Two hundred. Now that wouldn't be so tough. Four rich marks, less commission. Not too tough at all. But more likely it would be twenty come-and-go boys and in between there would be bread spent for rent, food, clothes and there she was back, again with nothing but crumbs in the purse. And if somewhere along the line she got a little too high or a little too drunk and found a nice soft-smiling one like Miles whom she liked, well then she'd find herself back with the razor and Freddie's finger—ah, why bother to think of it. It was a lousy world if you were broke or ugly. And sometimes not being ugly didn't help much.

But she was okay right now. Except that her heels were starting to eat through her foot. Well she had walked her five blocks so she could take her cab now.

She saw one at the curb, hurried to it, flung open the door and got in.

"Excuse me," said a woman with dark glasses and hair like melted gold, who was just paying the hack.

"Oh, I'm sorry," Allie said. "I didn't know—"

"That's all right," the woman said, taking off her glasses.

Allie felt the eyes meet hers, then sweep down her neck, to her breasts and then back up. The look embarrassed her more than she could ever remember being embarrassed before.

"I'm sorry," Allie said, getting up.

"No, sit," said the woman. "Maybe we can share the ride. Which way are you going?"

"Uptown," Allie said. "Way uptown."

"So am I," said the blonde with a smile. She sat back. "Give the man the address."

Allie did and the driver turned. He was a dense looking hefty man with a bulb nose.

"Ain't you getting out?" he said to the blonde. He looked at the change in his hand. "I thought—"

"I changed my mind," the woman said. "Drive on."

The hack shrugged, turned and shifted the gear. The cab pulled out into the wedge of uptown traffic.

"This is very nice of you," Allie said.

"It's my pleasure," said the woman. "My name's Roberta Wellins. Bobby to my friends."

"I'm Allie."

"Allie," the blonde said, turning the name over on her tongue. "Allie. I like that. Allie what?"

"Just Allie."

Roberta Wellins laughed. "Wonderful. Do you do anything, Allie? Are you married?"

"No and no," Allie said.

"Do you like men?"

The cabbie turned around and favored them with a confused stare.

"I like some men," Allie said.

"You don't mind me asking," Roberta Wellins said.

Allie shrugged. "Ask away."

"Wonderful. You see the reason I'm so curious is that I'm a doctor, a psychiatrist. That doesn't scare you, does it?"

"It might if I knew what it meant," Allie said.

Roberta laughed. "It would take too long to explain it all," she said. "But very simply put, a psychiatrist is concerned with what people are thinking. He likes to look into people's minds."

Allie raised an eyebrow.

"Does that sound odd to you?" Roberta asked.

"Yeah. A little, you know."

"I know. But you don't mind?"

"Baby," Allie said, relaxing now, "there's no place of mine that somebody hasn't looked already."

The cabbie turned again, naturally.

"I think we're getting along fine," Roberta said with a smile. "Do you have someplace particular to go now or would you like to have lunch with me?"

"I'm tapped," Allie said bluntly.

"I don't think I understand," Roberta said.

"I'm flat, baby. I got no bread for eats. I'm busted."

"Oh," said Roberta. "Well, my treat then. You can repay me by answering a few of my questions, if you *don't* think they're too personal."

"I've done more than answer questions to get a meal," Allie said.

Roberta laughed again.

Man, Allie thought, there ain't nothing that don't convulse this chick. I wonder what kind of stuff she takes.

They ate at a sidewalk restaurant on lower Fifth Avenue. White table cloths, clean silverware and a small bowl of fresh flowers in the center. Allie was impressed. She looked at the people passing and the people looked at her. Of course she had been on Fifth Avenue before but always walking, fast, with her head up and her eyes almost closed. Putting the dog on for the people who put the dog on. Showing them that she was as good as they were. But she had never seen it from a close vantage point before and it dazzled her.

So did the menu. It was mostly in French. She looked confused and she showed it.

"Would you like me to order for both of us?" Roberta asked.

"Please," Allie said, putting all the class she could muster into the word.

They had Manhattans before the meal. Allie would have preferred something with more punch and less sugar but Roberta ordered them before she could object.

They had another round of Manhattans with the meal which seemed to Allie to be mostly sauce over an inconsequential piece of meat and nothing but grass and fancy dressing for a salad.

They had a third round of Manhattans after the meal. And all the time, they had questions. Roberta asked her where she was born and what her parents were like; when she had moved to the city and if she liked it; where she lived and where she had worked; what her friends did and what her hobbies were.

It seemed to Allie to be just like one of those interviews in the movie magazines. Only a little different; because on the third Manhattan, Roberta's questions became a little more personal.

She prefaced the first one with, "Now if you don't want to answer this, dear, just say so and I'll shut up," and then she asked, "Are you a virgin?"

Allie had trouble keeping a straight face. "I'm afraid I'm not," she said, lowering her eyes.

"Would you mind telling me about it?"

Allie didn't mind. There wasn't very much to tell. It had happened when they were living in North Florida, when she was fifteen. Her father had a ribs-and-chicken stand, a kitchen with a small room in the back. She was minding the stand alone one day when a boy about eighteen came by. She had seen him around before and he had seen her but they had never talked. She took one look at him then and knew there wasn't going to be any talking at that time either. He didn't want any ribs; he wanted chicken. He came in, grabbed her by the wrist and pulled her in the back room.

For a few minutes she let him have his way, enjoying the way he touched her. It felt soft and warm. Then he touched her a new way and she screamed but his hand was over her mouth. She bit it, hard, and kept biting until he was finished. Then he got up and left. That was all. She didn't tell her folks; there was nothing to tell. They had expected it would happen sooner or later. They didn't really care as long as she didn't get pregnant. If she did, they would have to go hunting for the boy. Or somebody else. She didn't get pregnant.

"How horrid," Roberta said. "What a traumatic experience."

"Yeah," Allie said.

"Did you suffer any after-affects?"

"Uh-uh, I just washed up good like I was taught and nothing ever came of it."

"How did that affect your later experiences with men? Did you find yourself shying away from them?"

"I wouldn't say that exactly," Allie said with a broad smile.

The waiter came with the check.

"Would you like to go over to my apartment and finish this conversation?" Roberta asked with a smile.

"Sure," Allie said. "Long as I don't get caught for the cab fare."

Roberta laughed and this time Allie laughed too. She was beginning to feel good. Never would have believed those sugar drinks could do so much, she thought. She felt herself getting nice and loose and easy. In the cab, she rested her head back on the seat and answered Roberta's questions in a slow, languid drawl. She felt tired and several times her eyes began to close.

Her eyes opened wide, however, when she saw the apartment building. It was on Park Avenue, naturally, and looked a mile wide and two miles high. Allie had passed buildings like it a hundred times but she had always thought that they were office buildings. This one definitely wasn't. You could have fit a whole office in the building's lobby. It was all glass and mirrors and marble columns and even a small goldfish pond that someone had taken the goldfish from and almost filled with pennies.

"Hey," Allie said. "Somebody broke their piggy bank."

The apartment was even bigger than the lobby. A long hall filled with crazy-looking paintings led to a living room that sunk down two steps and then up three. There was a long turquoise sofa and two wild red chairs and two wilder green ones and a coffee table you could have played ping-pong on and a built-in wall of books.

Roberta pushed one of the books and two shelves slid away and a bar came out.

"Crazy," Allie said. "Chick, you've got the coolest pad that I've ever seen."

Roberta made them two drinks and then showed Allie the rest of it. It seemed to go on forever. There was a dining room with peppermint striped wallpaper and a table which Allie thought, but did not say, could have seated all the men she had ever laid. There was a kitchen that almost blinded her when the lights reflected off all the porcelain-and-chrome appliances. There was a study, all in black, lined with wine-colored books, and a desk the size of a bed and the biggest television set in the world. There was a bathroom where you could step into the tub and keep running for a few yards before you hit the wall and finally, there was a bedroom, all in yellow. Yellow walls, a giant double yellow bed, two yellow dressers, a yellow dressing table with a yellow stool before it. Over the bed was a painting, all yellow except for a fuzzy black spot in the center. Allie studied it for a minute, sipping her drink.

"Cool," was her verdict. She turned. "Baby, you've got it made, don't you. Man, I hate to think what you have to do to earn a pad like this. Don't tell me you get it just for asking all those silly questions?"

"Not just for asking," Roberta said. "Come, sit down." She patted the bed beside her. "Do you want another drink?"

"I wouldn't mind but I'd hate to have you make the trip."

"I'll be right back," Roberta said.

Allie stretched out on the bed. Man, she felt so cool. Oh, was this ever a pad or was this ever a pad? And this chick was okay too. If she could ever get off that question kick.

Roberta returned with the drinks and they finished them quickly.

"More questions now, I bet," Allie said.

"If you don't mind," Roberta said.

"1 don't mind if I don't have to get up."

"No, please. Make yourself comfortable."

Allie did just that. She crawled up to the pillow, wrapped her arms around it, brought her knees up and closed her eyes. "Fire away," she said.

"Do you have any favorite spots?" Roberta asked quietly.

"Uh-uh," Allie said.

"Did you understand my question?" Roberta asked.

"Uh-huh. Any favorite spots. They're all okay with me," she said languidly.

"Do you like to have your breasts touched?"

"Uh-huh."

"Kissed?"

"Umm."

"Do you like to have your nipples bitten?"

"Umm," Allie answered, half-asleep.

"And what about here?" Roberta said, sliding her hand under Allie's skirt and reaching up to touch and caress.

But by then, Allie was asleep.

She did not know how long she slept. But when she awoke she felt more tired than ever before. She yawned open-mouthed, still not aware of where she was, opened her eyes and saw the tips of her fingers and followed down, to her bare arm, to her shoulder, to her naked breasts, down, down, down.

She was completely nude.

She started awake and the next thing she saw was Roberta, nude also, lying beside her, her hand resting gently on Allie's buttocks. She moved the hand away carefully. The woman didn't stir, sleeping soundly, smiling.

Shaking her head to clear it, Allie got up. She saw her clothes piled neatly on the bench before the dressing table and on the way to them, she passed the mirror and caught a glimpse of herself.

At first she thought she was bleeding. At second look, she realized that it was lipstick.

Man, she thought. Man, little Allie had really fallen into it this time. Allie in wonderland.

She dressed hurriedly, keeping her eyes on the blonde woman.

She was a real beauty, Allie thought. No doubt about that. A real sleek white cat. All that long blonde hair, soft shoulders, big milk-white breasts with cherry-red nipples the size of half-dollars, sleek thighs and perfect legs.

A real beauty, Allie thought. And queer as a square egg. What a waste, she thought. But she didn't stop dressing to think because she felt she had to get out of there as fast as possible.

The blonde had not moved when Allie had finished dressing. Crossing to the door, Allie turned and gave her one last look. She was still smiling like a cat.

Man, Allie thought. I don't want to ever know what she did to me to make her smile like that.

Then she saw the jewel case on the dresser. It was open and the sunlight lancing through the blinds made the contents blaze like a flare. Allie walked over, took out a long shimmering necklace that glistened with tears. She looked over at the woman and then back at the necklace.

You might be a hooker, she said to herself, but you're not a thief. She looked at the necklace again and then put it in her purse. You might be a thief, she said as she hurried down the hall, but you're not stupid.

She caught the elevator and a cab who drove her uptown and waited outside while she talked to the fence. Then he drove her to the airport and during the whole ride, she kept on singing:

"Bye-bye, gay girl, bye-bye Freddie,

"Haiti, here I come."

Chapter 3

When she yawned and stretched and opened her eyes it was evening. Seven-thirty, according to the clock on the dresser. She squinted at the clock, noted the time, then rolled slowly over and tried to get back to sleep. She lay there with her face buried in the pillow, feeling soft and warm and happy, and then when sleep didn't come she yawned again and stretched again and got out of bed.

The Negro girl was gone. That was to be expected, she thought, and it was just as well. The libido could sweep you up and carry you along, but afterward it helped if you had something to talk about. Allie was a delight, but she had the feeling that she and Allie would have run out of things to talk about before long. So it was just as well that the girl had dressed and left.

She left the big yellow bedroom and went into the huge bathroom, ran warm water in the tub, added scented bath oil. She got into the tub and soaked in the water, feeling her body go limp as impotence. The water covered her to the neck, and the perfume of the bath oil was heady, intoxicating. She closed her eyes and relaxed.

You've done it again, she thought. You stupid oversexed tramp, you've gone and done it again.

Damn it, she thought. The water flowed over her, warmed her, soothed her. She let her hands run over her body. She massaged herself, squeezing her soft flesh, cupping her breasts and pinching her nipples.

Stop, she thought. You'll get yourself all excited again, and you'll jump out of the tub and go on the prowl. You'll pick another dark-skinned whore off the streets and take her to bed. Suppose she *was* a whore? Suppose she had syphilis, or gonorrhea, or something? That would be cute, all right.

She laughed. The laughter echoed, bouncing off the bathroom walls, and then died.

Roberta Wellins, M.D. Seventeen years of growing up in Forest Hills. (A baseball glove for Christmas? Are you sure, Bobby? Wouldn't you rather have a doll or something, honey?) Four years pre-med at NYU. (Listen, Bobby, don't be a nut. A girl can't be a doctor. It's a man's world, honey. Look, be a nurse, it's easier, you don't have so many years of studying, the work's the same. Then, if you want, you can *marry* a doctor!) Four years at Columbia Med School. Four years of specialized training. A year at the Sorbonne, studying under Fleischmann. Two years at a clinic in Chicago where the head resident kept making passes at her. (For Christ's sake, Wellins, you're going to give in sooner or later. Why not now? You gay or something, Wellins?)

And three years of private practice. She was thirty-four now, she was established and, most important, she was fashionable. They stretched out on her couch for fifty dollars an hour, and begged her to take them on for analysis. And the money rolled in. It was nice to have, money was. One could surround one's self with the little status symbols, one could grow happily accustomed to luxury. It was fine.

It would have been one thing if money were the most important factor. It was not. Roberta Wellins, M.D., was a dedicated psychiatrist. She believed in what she was doing. Of course, one can believe just as thoroughly at ten dollars an hour as at fifty, but conversely one can believe as well at fifty as at ten. Rejecting the money would only be an indication of disbelief in self, of guilt feelings, something like that. And ten dollars an hour would not pay the rent.

Roberta Wellins, M.D. Psychiatrist. Lesbian.

She sighed. Physician, heal thyself, she thought. Analyst, analyze thyself. Dyke, go to Denmark. You're a mess, Bobby Wellins. You pick whores off the street and ply them with liquor and seduce them after they're unconscious, and then you go around trying to help other neurotics straighten themselves out. You're a textbook case, Dr. Bobby.

She lolled in the tub, trying for the hundredth time to decide just where it had all started. A standard syndrome back in Forest Hills, the drunk and ineffectual father who inherited money and lapped it up; the domineering and extra-loving mother who held the family together. The old Oedipus complex turned inside-out, with Bobby Girl equipped with a big thing for Mama and nothing at all for Daddio.

Sure, you could start there. One beginning's as good as the next, all things considered. So start there. Move through the tomboy stage, which can be more of a stage when you've got the right personality to work with. Then land in the awkward adolescent stage, and if you're awkward enough you can parlay it into a scene. She had been awkward enough, by God. She was beautiful now, lithe and lovely. But in high school her face had been one big pimple, her legs had been matchsticks, her breasts had barely existed.

Then college at NYU in Washington Square, a Village pickup sooner or later, and away we go.

She remembered the first time. She'd finished the day's last class, then took a walk down Macdougal Street. There was a bar there, a loud place called the Swing Rendezvous, closed now after two dykes played games with knives and one of them wound up dead. It was open then, and as far as she knew at the time it was a bar like any other. She went in, ordered a drink, sat sipping it and listening to the jukebox.

Hell, drop the naïveté bit. Halfway through the drink she had the place figured out. When you see nothing but girls in a bar, when half of them have shortie haircuts and wear pants and shirts, when they dance with each other, you have to be from a small town in Kansas to miss the message. She was from Queens, which wasn't exactly a small town in Kansas, though it sometimes tried to be. She didn't miss the connection.

When the brunette asked her to dance, she danced.

When the brunette asked her to leave, she left. Hand in happy hand with the brunette, who gave her hand a squeeze now and then in case there was a message she had missed.

There wasn't.

The brunette was named Lou. She lived on Barrow Street in a third-floor walk-up with cockroaches. Bobby wasn't used to cockroaches. After the third drink she didn't mind them. She didn't notice them, actually, because she was too busy noticing other things.

Like Lou.

For example.

Like how she felt when Lou touched her breasts, and like how she felt when Lou's lips blazed a trail of kisses along her body. Like Lou's breasts against her own breasts, Lou's warm mouth kissing her own just-as-warm mouth . . .

Things like that.

The world pulse-beating crazily, building up for something she had never known about. Explosions, and starbursts, and all of it. The works, spread out on a dirty bed in a roachy room on Barrow Street. The whole shooting match, better than the books had said it could be, better than her imagination had ever imagined.

"You're one of us now," Lou had told her. "You're a lesbian, Bobby. Don't ever forget it."

Forget? How?

"There are girls who like men and girls who like girls. We can't help being the way we are. You can't help it. Believe me, it's better that way. We don't get pregnant, we don't get married, we don't wind up tied to a sink and a dishwasher and some man's zipper. We don't get trapped, Bobby."

I'm trapped already, she thought but did not say. I'm trapped already.

She stayed in the trap. She finished at NYU and went on to med school at Columbia, and she moved from Forest Hills then because you couldn't spend two to three hours commuting with all the work they piled on you at med school. She took a furnished room on the Upper West Side, studied night and day, and went to the Village whenever she had some free time. A night, a few hours, an hour. A trip to the Swing Rendezvous, a lustful but loveless pickup, a wink and a dance and a kiss . . .

Some lesbians fell in love. She was not one of them. For her, sex was on a single plane, a physical phenomenon to be taken when needed. Emotions had little to do with it. It helped if you liked the person you were in bed with. But that was as far as it went. Hardly a healthy attitude. Hardly in keeping with the best of contemporary psychiatric thinking.

The years in Chicago were hell, not only because of the pass-tossing resident but because it took her awhile before she found out where the gay clubs were. And then she got involved, met a girl who fell hard for her. A borderline paranoid, a redheaded hypothyroid type with wild eyes and wilder breasts. Sandra, by name. The affair with Sandra lasted four months; she kept it up because she was afraid the girl would commit suicide or murder if she broke it off. And then, ultimately, she did break it off. And Sandra came at her with a knife, a big wicked carving knife.

God, how she hated knives! Symbolic, of course. Fear of intercourse, fear of men, fear of discovery, fear of everything. Which was nice to know, but which still left her crazy-scared of knives. She had taken that one away from Sandra, walked out and left her. Sandra had used another knife, a paring knife, to slash her wrists. She bled to death and Bobby cowered and waited for the scandal.

It never came. Paris next, the Sorbonne, the French girls. The States again, private practice, and away we go on the money tree.

Physician, heal thyself. She could analyze, she could play question and answer games, she could treat and prescribe. She was good with her patients. She got results.

But she couldn't do much for herself.

She got out of the tub, rubbed her body dry until her skin

ached from the brisk massage. She fingered her breasts, rubbed her thighs. Guilt, she thought, and nothing but. Punishing yourself with a rubdown for the fun you had this afternoon. Good thinking, Dr. Bobby.

Guilt was a rare commodity lately. If you were that way, and if you appeared destined to remain that way, you either learned to overcome it or you cut your wrists. If you were going to be gay, you had to adjust to it. Otherwise you were in a bad spot.

She went into the bedroom and got dressed. She put on a bra, underwear, garter belt and stockings, a tailored flannel suit. She brushed her blonde hair diligently, then wrapped it up in a French roll. She slipped her feet into high heels and went to her jewelry box to pick out a pair of earrings. Then she noticed that the necklace was gone. Allie, she thought. Allie, Allie, did you have to rob me? And, for God's sake, did you have to take something so expensive? The necklace had cost twenty-five hundred dollars. It would be sorely missed.

Insurance, she thought. Did it cover her? It did. And suppose they investigated, and suppose they found out how it had been stolen and by whom, and suppose—

Now you're getting paranoid, she told herself. They'll investigate, and then they'll pay the claim. And that's all. There was nothing to worry about.

Oh, Allie, she thought. A twenty-five hundred dollar necklace. And now you'll sell it to some crooked pawnbroker for four or five hundred, and you'll give the money to a vicious Harlem pimp. I'd have given you money, Allie, if knew you wanted it. I'd have given you anything—

She shrugged the little mental speech away. She was hungry,

very hungry. She had eaten nothing since lunch. She could cook something, of course. The kitchen made cooking sterilely simple, aseptically easy. But she hated to cook, hated to wash clothes, hated to do any feminine tasks. Typical, she thought, very typical.

She took a cab to a Hungarian restaurant on Second Avenue in the Eighties and ordered chicken paprikash. She ate slowly, enjoying her food, smoked three cigarettes and drank four cups of coffee after dinner. The bath had left her feeling limp and listless, but the meal pepped her up and the coffee got her blood circulating again. When she had finished the fourth cup of coffee she paid the check and left a tip. She lit another cigarette and left the restaurant.

Then she remembered something.

She had a date.

A vague date, anyway. She had been walking on Third Avenue a day or two ago, browsing in antique shops and met a girl. A dark-haired girl, young, lovely. And because she was not the fall-in-love type of dyke, but the lecherous-hit-and-runner, she had made a pass at the girl. It was laughable, in a way. The girl was no lesbian, not by a long shot. Although she might have possibilities. She was about sixteen or seventeen, blue-jeaned and Celanese-jacketted, pony-tailed and thrusting-breasted, and Bobby had struck up a conversation with her. She'd bought the girl a coke in a candy store, then suggested the girl come up to her apartment.

"I got things to do," the girl had said.

"A boy friend?"

"No."

"You must have a lot of boy friends."

"Not so many."

"A girl has to be careful with boys. They're only after one thing, you know."

And more of the same. And, finally, a date to meet at nine or ten in front of the same candy store. The date was for tonight, and she barely had time to make it.

She found herself striding along, cutting west to Third, heading downtown a block or two toward the candy store. Ridiculous, she thought. You don't need it now, you had it with Allie and it already cost you a necklace. You're crazy, Dr. Bobby, and you'll get yourself in trouble. The girl is underage. For Freud's sake, be careful, be sensible, be—

Be damned, she thought. It didn't work that way. The fact that you'd had sex recently did nothing to calm a good strong lech. She remembered a girl named Connie Lingus, an hourglass shaped bisexual girl who was ready to go any time, and for anybody. Was she getting to be like that? Maybe she was—it certainly looked that way.

The girl was waiting for her in front of the candy store. She was smiling warily, and Bobby couldn't see her eyes. A poor disturbed youth, she thought. The kind you straighten out on a couch, not in bed. Now you'll ruin the kid for life, Dr. Bobby. You'll damage her psyche permanently. You'll make a dyke out of her.

She couldn't help it.

"Hello," she said gently. "I'm sorry if I'm late."

"It's okay."

"Would you like a coke? Or some coffee?"

"No thanks."

"We could taxi to my apartment," she said. "It's not far from here, and you could have a drink."

"There's a place near here," the girl said.

Bobby looked at her.

"Listen," the girl said, "you think I don't know what you want? You think I'm a sap? You want me, lady. You want to see if I feel as good as I look. You want to play with me. Right?"

She looked away. Her face was flaming—she could feel her cheeks burning—and suddenly she envied Allie. Allie couldn't blush.

"It's okay," the girl said. "I don't mind."

"I—"

"Only I don't want to go to your place," the girl said. "I got a place, a room around the corner. We can go there."

She followed the girl around the corner, halfway down the block. The side streets were shabbier than Third Avenue, not exactly slum-level, more lower middle-class. The girl stopped at a red brick building and led the way down a flight of stone steps to the basement.

"In here," she said.

"Here?"

"It's a sort of a club," the girl said.

In the doorway, while the girl was fitting a key into a lock, Bobby kissed her. She didn't want to, wanted to wait until they were inside. But she couldn't help herself. She grabbed the girl by the shoulders, spun her around, covered her mouth with her own mouth, sank her tongue between the girl's lips. A sweet mouth, a mouth tasting of Coca-Cola and cigarettes. Breasts she could feel through the Celanese jacket.

God—

The girl stiffened slightly. Then she pulled away, turned the key in the lock and pushed the door open. The room was dark.

"Go on," the girl said.

Bobby walked into the room. Behind her the girl was closing the door. She was nervous now. Why weren't there any lights?

Then there were lights.

Then she saw them.

Eight of them, all dressed alike in black leather jackets and skin-tight dungarees. Boys, sixteen or eighteen years old, with cruel mouths and bright eyes. They were looking at her and she was terrified.

And the girl was saying: "Take good care of this bitch, Tony. The goddamned dyke kissed me on the way in. She's a real pig, Tony."

Tony said: "Beat it."

The girl opened the door, went out. One of the other boys went to the door and latched it. She looked at Tony. He was the tallest one, the heaviest one, probably the oldest. He had his hands on his hips, and there was a cigarette hanging from the corner of his mouth.

"You rotten dyke," he said. "This time you're gonna catch it."

She stared.

"Messing around with a broad like Brenda. Trying to make a dyke out of her. You'll catch it, bitch."

She looked around. The room was barely furnished. There was a sagging bed along one wall, a few chairs, a table holding a cheap record player. There were pictures of naked girls on the wall, some of them torn from magazines, others frankly pornographic.

There was no place to run, no place to hide.

"Please," she said.

Tony laughed.

"Please—"

He advanced on her, eyes veiled. His hand shot out suddenly, fingers extended, stabbing into her soft belly. The pain was like a knife in her stomach and she doubled over in agony. He slapped her then, forehand and backhand, forehand and backhand, until she thought her head was going to come off.

"Please—"

He spun on his heel, pointed a forefinger at each of two boys. "Hold her," he said. "Grab the bitch by the arms and hold onto her. We teach this one a lesson. We work her over so she knows to keep her hands off decent young kids like Brenda."

They held her. They moved toward her, one on each side, and they gripped her upper arms so tightly that her fingers went numb. And then Tony crashed a fist into her breast.

She would have fallen if they hadn't been holding her. She would have fallen again when he punched her other breast. But instead she moaned, saw stars and flashes, finally screamed. He cut off the scream by sending his fist into her open mouth. A tooth fell out. She licked her lips and tasted blood, and her eyes began to tear.

He stopped, finally. He stepped back, and she thought that it was all over, that they were letting her go. I've learned my lesson, fellows, she thought. I'll confine myself to professional prostitutes and card-carrying lesbians, I'll leave virgins like Brenda alone, just let me go, just let me alone, just let me out of here—

He put his hand into his pocket. He brought out a knife,

flicked it open. The blade was six inches long and she shrieked when she saw it.

A knife. Like the knife Sandra had come at her with, like the knife Sandra had slashed her wrists with. A knife, moving toward her now, a knife, a knife—

"Gonna strip you," Tony said. "Gonna cut your fancy dyke clothes off you."

The knife popped the buttons from the suit jacket. One by one the buttons popped off, clattered onto the floor. Then Tony stepped back and the two boys holding her arms ripped the jacket off.

Then the blouse.

Then the bra.

And Tony was saying: "Hey, the dyke's got breastworks! You catch that, boy? Go ahead grab a feel."

They touched her, squeezed her, pinched her. She felt their dirty hands kneading her flesh, tugging painfully at her nipples. Her breasts ached from the beating Tony had given her and the mauling was even worse. She wanted to cry.

"Rotten dyke," he said; "I oughta cut 'em off of you."

Instead he cut off the skirt and the garter belt and the panties. He picked up her feet one at a time and yanked her shoes off. She stood naked in front of him and he put the sharp tip of the knife into her navel. He pressed, slightly, and a bead of red blood appeared.

"I oughta stick it in all the way," he said.

She couldn't breathe.

"Shank and Bobo and Kenny," he said. "Get her over to the

bed and tie her up. Tie her up good. Use her bra and that garter thing and make sure she can't wiggle worth a damn."

She tried to struggle but it didn't work. They were stronger than she was. They dragged her across the rough wooden floor to the bed and they threw her down on the bed on her stomach.

"Roll her over," she heard Tony say. "I want to work on her for awhile."

They rolled her over. She was lying on her back and they were lashing her to the bed posts, tying her wrists and ankles so that she was spread-eagled on the bed and could not move. Tony ripped friction tape from a roll, plastered it over her mouth. She tried to breathe through her mouth. The gag was airtight.

"Somebody gimme a belt," Tony said.

Somebody gave him a belt, a heavy garrison belt with a steel buckle. He swung the belt high over his head and she stared at it, eyes wide in horror. He brought it down with all his strength across her bare belly and she screamed into the gag. The belt went up again, came down again. She writhed like a snake and her whole stomach felt as though it were on fire.

"Careful," somebody was saying. "You'll kill the broad."

"That's the breaks."

"You can't kill her yet. Not till we get our kicks."

"I'm getting my kicks now," Tony said. "Watch!"

The belt came down on her breasts. She thought she was going to pass out from the pain but she couldn't black out. She remained conscious while he lashed at her again and again with the heavy belt until her breasts were two slabs of raw meat.

"Jesus," he said, "she squirms nice."

"You know it, Tony."

"I wonder," he said thoughtfully. "Suppose I dropped a butt between those tits of hers and let her squirm. How long you figure it would take for her to squirm it off of there?"

"Just a second or two," somebody said.

"Maybe a minute."

"Half a minute. Thirty seconds."

No, she thought. No. Please, no!

"I wonder," Tony said. "I think we should find out. Like a scientific experiment. So we beat the Russians and everything. Somebody gimme a cigarette."

Somebody gave him a cigarette. She watched him snap a match to light it with elaborate ease. Then he grinned an ugly grin at her and held the cigarette an inch from her eye.

"Listen, dyke," he said. "We're having this experiment. I'm gonna stick this between those boobs, see, and then you gotta squirm. We'll see how long it takes. Somebody time this, dammit."

No. No, no, no!

He put the cigarette between her breasts. For a second she lay still with the shock. The cigarette was burning her, hurting her, and she started to writhe, twisting against the cords that were holding her to the bed. The cigarette slid downward to her stomach, went to the left, skidded back toward the center. She smelled her skin burning and the tears flowed freely from her eyes now. It was horrible.

And then, finally, the cigarette was gone. "A minute and seven seconds," somebody said.

"That ain't too fast."

"Maybe we should let her try to break her record, Tony."

"Naw," he said. "I got better things for this broad to do. Better things."

She opened her eyes. It didn't take her long to guess what better things he had on the agenda. A mass rape.

The rotten little sadists. Disturbed kids—that's what they were supposed to be. Disturbed? They were rotten. What did they want from her?

Sex, for the time being. Tony, the leader, went first. And she steeled herself for it, waited, knew better than to fight it. She was ready, he was hurting her.

It was worse than hell.

It was worse than anything. She had never had sex with a man, had never had anything to do with men. It was awful. She felt her whole body being torn in two, felt herself writhing and twisting with pain. It went on halfway to forever. When it was over she closed her eyes and passed out.

When she came to again, somebody else was in Tony's place. She was barely aware of pain or of anything else. I'm dead, she thought. I died a long time ago. None of this is really happening to me. It's a dream, a nightmare.

But wasn't it ever going to end?

Not right away, anyhow. Because they all took their turns with her, one at a time, with Tony and a boy called Shank having seconds. Periodically she would pass out; periodically she would regain consciousness again. It didn't seem to matter to them whether she was awake or asleep, alive or dead. They were not human beings; they were animals, using her body viciously and dispassionately and horribly.

Tony said: "Anybody want more?"

Nobody did.

"Let her go," somebody said. "She won't try anything now. She's learned, Tony."

"I don't know," he said.

"Let her go, man."

"I don't see letting her go. Suppose she calls the cops? We're in a bind."

"No dyke's gonna call no cops, Tony."

"I don't know," he said. "You never know with a dyke. She might get some of her butch friends and try to give Brenda a hard time. Or she might go to the cops after all. Once a dyke, always a dyke. The only way to get rid of 'em is to kill 'em."

Silence. She shuddered. Don't do it, she thought. Don't—I'm still alive, I'm beaten and broken but alive. Don't take all I've got away from me. Please, I'm alive, I'm alive, let me live.

Tony flicked the knife open. She looked at it and shivered.

"Not that stuff, Tony. We never killed nobody yet."

"We gotta start sometime."

"We done bad things, Tony. Nothing like killing."

"So?"

"Don't kill her, man."

The knife moved toward her and she stared at it in horror. The blade was very sharp, very shiny. He held it to her throat and she could not breathe or move.

"The hell," he said.

The knife dipped suddenly. The tip of the blade flicked gently across her right breast, soft as a caress, leaving a thin red line of blood on the white flesh. Then the knife slashed through the cords that were holding her in position. She felt hands tugging at her, hands pulling her.

"If she's a dyke," Tony said, "she oughta dress like one. Let's fix her up with a wardrobe."

They dressed her in a pair of dungarees with nothing under them and the denim chafed her groin. They added a black leather jacket over her bare breasts. The boy called Shank zipped it for her. Then they were shoving her toward the stairs, pushing her out the door and up to the street. When they let go of her she pitched forward on her face.

"Up, dyke!"

He writes for the *New Yorker,* she thought. Then she got on all fours, her whole body a sheet of pain, and began to crawl away.

Chapter 4

The center fold of the *Daily News* had a large photograph of a newly arrived Italian siren leaning over a ship's railing, waving her breasts at the crowd. Tony's eyes lingered over it.

"Who's that?" Shank asked.

"Some Guinea tart," Tony said, flipping the page.

"Lemme see."

"Later." His eyes roamed up and down the columns of type. He turned another page and then he was past the news section. "It's not in," he said. "Unless it's in the women's section." He grinned.

"Lemme check," Shank said.

Tony balled the paper together and tossed it toward a garbage can ten feet from them. The ball unraveled in the air and the papers scattered like leaves down Third Avenue.

"It's been three days," Shank said. "You think maybe she didn't ring the cops?"

"Why should she?" Tony said, reaching over to take a pack of cigarettes from Shank's pocket. He put one in his mouth and the pack in his own pocket. "We probably gave her the biggest kick of her life. Maybe even straightened her out for good. I wouldn't be surprised if she came looking for us to give us a reward."

"Gimme my butts back," Shank said. "That's my last pack."

"Go roll a spade."

"Come on," Shank said insistently. "You can cop all you want at work. I gotta go looking for mine."

Tony gave him an eloquent one finger reply and started sauntering down Third, kicking at the newspapers as he came to them.

"You gonna go to work today?" Shank said, walking beside him.

"I ain't decided yet."

"It's almost ten, you know. Old man Fortuna will kick your tail in if you cut out again."

"Let him try," Tony said. "I've been looking for a reason to open him up. Let him just look cross-eyed at me once more and I'll run him through his own grinder."

Shank laughed accommodatingly. "Hey listen," he said, "you gonna get the stuff for the boys tomorrow? You promised it for last Friday, you know."

"I told you The Wig didn't show. If he shows tomorrow, I'll get some from him."

"How much? Two ozees?"

"Maybe. Maybe even four if I got the bread."

"You gonna cut it? Kenny and Bobo said you been cutting the stuff. They said it don't smoke the same no more."

Tony exhaled a thin stream of smoke. "They ain't told me that. You tell them, they got any bitch come see me."

"I told them that," Shank said. "That's just what I said to them. I told them I didn't know nothing about it, I wasn't even there when you rolled the joints. Hell they smoke the same to me."

"That's good," Tony said.

"You ain't been cutting them, have you?" Shank asked, nervously.

"You accusing me?" Tony asked, stopping.

"No. Hell, no. I was just wondering, that's all." He looked away from Tony's stare. "Wouldn't make no difference to me even if you were. I told you they smoke the same."

"No problems then," Tony said, walking on. "Everybody's swinging. Let Kenny and Bobo get their own if they're not flying. I think Kenny's been popping on the side anyway, that's why the joints aren't flipping him."

"Where could he get junk? You figure The Wig's pushing that too?"

Tony shrugged. "I ain't interested in knowing. He's got hash though. He told me about that."

"You gonna get some for the boys?"

Tony blew a perfect smoke ring. "Uh-uh. They wouldn't appreciate it. I might get some for me though."

"And me," Shank said. "I ain't never blew hash. Get some for me, too, Tony, all right?"

"Hash costs big. You got the bread?"

"I'll get it. I'll get it today. My old lady gets paid today and I found out where she's stashing it again."

"Where?" Tony asked casually.

"Behind the stove. You gotta disconnect the whole thing to get to it."

"Smooth place. I'll have to remember that."

"You wouldn't cop it first, would you, Tony? Come on, you wouldn't do that."

"Course not," Tony said with a grim smile. "But I figure I got a right to if I wanted. Since I ain't got an old lady of my own, it's only fair that I get to cop from yours once in a while. Don't that sound right to you?"

The logic momentarily puzzled Shank. His blond eyebrows knit in confusion and his pocked face looked blank.

"Don't sweat it," Tony said, flicking his butt at a passing car. "If I decide to do it, you'll be the first one I tell."

Shank looked relieved.

They walked on. In the second doorway from the corner, Tony spied an old rheumy looking bum crouched, sleeping fitfully with an unfinished pint in his hands.

"Want a drink?" he asked Shank.

"Sure," Shank said. "I mean, you're gonna have one, aren't you?"

"Why not? Best thing for breakfast. Go get it."

Shank walked over quietly, suppressing a giggle, and carefully slipped the bottle from the bum's hands. The man mumbled something incoherent and a froth of spittle leaked from the corner of his mouth. His head of scab-matted white hair lolled to his shoulder and he awoke with a twitch.

"Hey," he said, focusing on Shank who was just skipping backward with the pint in his hand. "Hey, you, what you doin'?" He pulled himself to his feet.

"Kick him," Tony said.

Shank kicked him, the toe of his boot catching the bum in the shoulder and crashing him back against the doorway. He slumped in the corner, made a token effort to rise and then collapsed, staring at them vacantly.

"Good point," Tony said, walking on.

Shank smiled. "Here." He offered the bottle.

"You first," Tony said.

Shank tilted the greasy unlabeled pint and let three swallows of the auburn liquid gurgle down his throat. "Here," he said breathily.

"You had enough?" Tony asked.

Tony took the bottle, looked at it and then hurled it against the building wall. It shattered in a dozen twinkling shards.

"I wouldn't drink that stuff if you paid me," he said.

Shank looked stunned and offended.

They turned the corner and Tony stopped in front of Fortuna's Market and looked at the chained delivery cart at the curb.

"You gonna work?" Shank asked.

"Yeah. I just decided. I'll see you tonight."

"Sure. All right." The blond boy dug his hands into his dungaree pockets, hunched his shoulders and walked off.

Tony lit a cigarette and pushed through the glass-and-wire-mesh door. About a dozen women were roaming the aisles of canned goods, boxes and vegetable bins; five more were lined up with their carts waiting to be checked out by Fortuna, a bald, pebble-eyed man whose gross body seemed painfully cramped in the register booth. He turned from his machine when he saw Tony.

"Hey, tough guy," he called loudly. "You working here nights now?"

Screw you, Tony thought; but he only said, "This the stuff to go?" gesturing at the five address-scrawled cartons near the door.

"No, those are Christmas presents for you," Fortuna said. The woman he was servicing tittered. Tony fixed her with a vicious stare and she turned away, coloring.

"Don't visit nobody," Fortuna said. "I want you back here before twelve."

Tony took the key from the wall hook, carried one of the cartons outside, unlocked the cart and dumped the box in. Something tinkled inside. Three more trips and the cart was loaded and he was pushing it down the street, avoiding the smiling glances of passers-by.

Tony Monto, delivery boy, he thought. He wanted to shove the cart into the gut of the next bustard that grinned at him. Lousy finks with their cruddy briefcases; fat-tailed broads with lemons down to their knees. He'd give them something to grin about. He'd take these goddamn celery stalks and ram them . . .

He gave the cart a vicious shove and it went wobbling down the street ahead of him.

Tony Score—like the boys called him because he could hammer a broad more times than they could count—that was more like it. Tony Score who led his boys to some real kicks. Like that dyke the other night. And like the pot he'd get from The Wig tomorrow, if he caught enough in tips today. If. If. If. The goddamn world was just one big stinking If. If he had enough bread, then he could fly. If his old man staggered across the street at the right time, maybe he'd get hit by a truck. If he walked into the wrong alley, maybe the Lords would be waiting to pay him back for what he did to their chief last week. If Brenda didn't have something on with her hot numbers man tonight, maybe he'd get into her pants.

If. And the bit with Brenda was a real gas. He had been the one to break her in first. He had noticed that she was filling out before anyone else knew she was a broad. He had taken her and showed her what loving was all about. And now she was copping out on him for some flat-nosed Spic.

She had begged for it so nice the other night. They were lying on the roof of her building and she had all of her clothes under her.

"Do it to me," she asked, squirming around.

"Pay attention to what you're doing," he said, squeezing her nipples.

"Come on, Tony. Please."

"No," he said.

"Ah, you're a fink."

His hand tightened on her nipple. "Say that again."

"Oww! That hurts."

"It's supposed to hurt. Now go ahead and do what I want you to do."

"All right. But let go."

He let go, keeping his hand on her breast just in case. But it wasn't necessary. She knew what the story was . . .

"That's it, baby," he said. "That's nice. That's nice."

And then he was rubbing his hands lovingly over her back, sliding down to smooth her buttocks, pinching until he felt himself beginning to groove, really groove.

"Oh you've got it now, baby," he said, writhing. "Oh now, doll. Now. Now. Now!" And then he couldn't speak any more because the pleasure was a hot wave spinning inside him, touching all of his nerves at once.

Crap! He pulled the cart to a stop in front of a dirty yellow tenement. Apartment 4-D read the last line of the address on the carton.

Four stinking flights, he thought as he lifted the box onto his shoulder and braced himself for the smell of the hallway. It still hit him like an old sock, getting worse as he went up. He jabbed at the bell of 4-D. Nothing. He pushed again.

Come on, you stupid bitch, he thought. You ordered this garbage now come get it.

On the third ring, the door opened and a frowsy looking woman wearing a housecoat open to the navel exposing her breasts—like fried eggs hanging on a hook—and flat bedroom slippers peered out at him.

"Fortuna's," Tony said.

"Just a minute," the woman said and closed the door.

Tony heard her yelling: "Nick, it's the food. You got a quarter for the kid?"

"No," Nick said. "Tell him we'll get him next time."

The woman was back at the door. "I got no change," she said, smiling. "We'll get you—"

"I heard," Tony said, setting the box down.

"Bring it into the kitchen," the woman said.

"Bring it in yourself, you rotten whore." He turned and walked down the stairs.

"You little punk!" the woman screamed after him. "Hey, Nick, did you hear what—"

The downstairs door closed on her sentence.

Nick heard, Tony thought. He'll get me next time. The bustard. What a stinking neighborhood. The bitch gets out of bed at eight o'clock, goes shopping and then comes back to dive into the sack for another round with Nick The Sport. Real class A finks.

The second delivery was no better. Same neighborhood, same

kind of building, same pukey smell. Only this time he knew the woman, a fat-boobed slob named Selaski who was usually good for a buck tip if he slipped his hand under her dress and gave her a goose. But this time she was busy with somebody else and he caught only a fat smile and a stinking dime.

"It's all I got now," she whispered as she led him out. "But why don't you come back a little later?"

"Yeah, I'll do that," Tony said. Yeah, sure, he thought. Later, man. It was an If and Later world with no locks in it. If you weren't sweating out one thing, you were sweating out another. And here was a big fat dime for his morning's work and where the hell was he going to get the bread to pay The Wig?

The rest of the day was not much better. By six when he was making his last run, he had netted a heavy four bills. Bat crap, he thought. It didn't even pay to work on Thursdays, nobody got their dough until tomorrow. It was just a big fat drag.

His last delivery changed his mind. The address was the only decent building in the area, a tenement that had been renovated and rewired. The front was smooth-blasted graystone and though there were still stairs and no elevator, the halls were clean and there were buzzers over the chromium mail slots. He pushed the one for 3-B, Cameron, and the drone sounded almost immediately. The carton was light and he took the stairs two at a time with the box in his hands. The door to 3-B was open when he got there. A young redheaded woman with a doll's face and the biggest bust Tony had ever seen pushing out a yellow sweater smiled at him.

"Would you bring it into the kitchen, please?" she asked, turning. Tony followed her, his eyes on her rear which swayed innocently under the tan skirt. Her legs were good, but not great; her body was well proportioned but her breasts—

She turned and those big hard lemons brushed against his arm. She seemed not to notice it.

"I'll have to get some change in the bedroom," she said and walked down a short hallway.

Tony waited, watching after her. The apartment was small: living room, kitchenette and the bedroom and bath. All modern furniture and clean. A short sofa, coffee table, two deep chairs. Tony looked around for something worth copping but nothing was in sight.

The redhead came back.

Jesus, Tony thought. Like goddamn basketballs. Mmm, would he like to sink his teeth into those. He guessed her nipples were the size of plates.

"I've just moved into this neighborhood," the redhead said, "and I'm afraid I don't know what to tip." She handed him a quarter and a dime. "Is that enough?" she asked.

"It's okay," Tony said, meeting her dark green eyes and then leaving them to return his gaze to her breasts.

She pulled embarrassedly at the bottom of her sweater. "Well, thank you very much," she said, turning to the door.

Tony didn't move. He stood, legs apart, one hand hooked in his belt loop, the other holding the change she had just given him.

"You live here alone?" he asked.

"Yes. Why?"

He shrugged. "No reason. You ever go out?"

"Yes," she said, coloring. "But I'm afraid I'm engaged if you were . . ." She let the sentence trail off.

"I wasn't thinking anything," Tony said, rolling the coins in his hand. "Why? You think I'm too young for you?"

"No," the girl said, nervously. "No, I just—well, I don't know. Would you please go now? I have to start preparing dinner."

"Why don't you ask me to have a drink?" Tony suggested.

"I'm afraid I can't. You see my fiancé should be arriving almost any minute now and he wouldn't—"

"I'll explain the whole bit to him," Tony said. "Don't sweat. Come on, break out the stuff. We'll swing a little."

"I'm afraid that's impossible," the girl said. "Look, would you please leave now. I don't want to have to call—"

"Cool it, baby," Tony said, palms raised. "I'm not out to hammer you." He walked toward her slowly and she opened the door, backing away.

Tony grinned. "You really got the shakes, chick. Here," he held out his hand. "Shake."

The girl drew back. "Really, I wish you'd—"

"No, baby. Gimme some skin. We'll make like friends."

Tremulously, the girl held out her hand. Tony's thick fingers closed around it and he pulled her slowly toward him.

"No," she said. "Please."

Grinning, he cupped his hand up and under her left breast and patted gently. "That's all," he said. "Just wanted to see if they were real."

The girl flushed crimson and pulled her hand back. "If you don't leave now, I'll call the police," she said.

"Sure, baby, sure. I'm gone." And he strolled out. Mamma, he thought, clicking down the stairs. I've got to cut myself a piece of that. Ummm! He pounded a fist into his palm. Little Tony has got to see those bombs in the flesh, he thought. I touched but I still don't believe. What a mouthful.

Passing the outside hallway, he took another look at the name-plate. 3-B, Cameron. You just keep them hanging there, baby, he thought. Little Tony is going to be back.

He came back at nine that night. He hadn't even bothered to ring Brenda. Hell, both of her breasts would make one of Cameron's. He thought about those breasts while he was eating dinner. Every time his mouth opened, he thought about those luscious pink mounds. He chewed on a mouthful of steak and thought about those giant red nipples that would probably be the size of pencils when they were up. All he wanted was to bury his head in those basketballs and kiss and bite and nuzzle.

At nine he was in the hallway, pressing the buzzer. This time there was no drone in return; instead a male voice came over the intercom.

"Yes. Who is it?"

Tony didn't bother to answer. So she wasn't putting him on about the fiancé, he thought walking out. She'd probably told the square what had happened, and that's why he was answering the buzzer. Well, he'd just take a look at the guy who was playing around with her first and then decide what to do.

He stood on the street and looked up at the gray façade of the building. No fire escapes in front. That meant that they had to be in the rear. Swinging. That's right where her bedroom was.

A low spiked gate guarded the alley which led to the back courtyard. Tony swung over it easily. Now which goddamn side is she on? he wondered. It took a minute to figure it out, another thirty seconds to determine the right apartment. He chinned himself up onto the first level of the fire escape and was up the orange steel steps like a cat. He paused on the second floor to look in on a couple watching a Western on television and then he was at her window.

Drapes.

Crap!

But the curtains didn't fit flush at the corners; squatting, he could see through into the dark vacant bedroom and beyond where the girl and her fiancé were sitting on the sofa necking.

She had changed into slacks but wore the same yellow sweater and the man's hand was on it now, rubbing gently, as his mouth engaged hers in an extended kiss.

Jesus, Tony thought. What I wouldn't give to be grabbing those now. Go on, square. Get yourself a handful for me.

But the fiancé seemed otherwise inclined. He removed his hand and broke the clinch; the couple smiled at each other and began talking.

Tony waited. He waited ten minutes and then twenty. And then another ten. But there was nothing to see. Periodically, the girl moved from the couch to get a cigarette or fix a new drink and every few minutes, the man leaned over to bestow a light kiss on her cheek but that was all.

Crap, Tony thought. Come on, square, get her in the goddamn bedroom. Tear off that sweater and that halter she must wear to keep those bombers in place and dig in.

The fiancé did not dig in. Tony waited, chain smoking cigarettes, and straining in his squat, and finally he gave up.

They're finished for the night, he decided, straightened up and went clicking down the fire escape steps.

He was too busy the next day to give the redhead much thought. He hustled like hell to make enough tips to pay The Wig for the pot. But at seven when he met him at Wendy's Drugs and Soda, he had collected only enough for an ounce.

"Your boys can't fly very high on that," The Wig said.

"The hell with the boys," Tony said. "This is all for me."

The Wig smiled. He was a hefty beet-faced man of about thirty, very Madison Avenue from his flat straw haircut to his De Vahni bronze-brown shoes. "Why not turn on with hash then?" he said.

"How much?"

"I could give you half an ounce instead of an ozee in pot."

"How many joints?"

"Depends," The Wig said. "You gonna cut it with oregano?"

"Uh-uh," Tony smiled. "I only do that for my boys. So they don't get sick."

The Wig grinned. "Make fifteen, maybe twenty joints then. But you can really score with these. If you don't want junk, this is the best."

"Okay," Tony said. "Go get it."

"Bread first," The Wig said.

Tony laughed. "Me pay front money? Come off it, man."

The Wig laughed. "Just checking. Sometimes I can cop out that way."

"Go get the stuff," Tony said.

The Wig was back in minutes. He kept the stuff in his car,

Tony knew, and one of these days he was going to have Shank keep The Wig busy while he went through that little short.

"Here you go, baby," The Wig said handing him a folded newspaper. "Fly high."

Tony paid him and went to his room. He wasn't worried about The Wig laying false on him. He was the only one who bought for that territory and The Wig wouldn't run the risk of losing the business, especially now when his boys were almost ready to graduate.

He spread the stuff out on the newspaper, flattened it evenly and separated it into small piles. Twenty joints, hell! He'd have to pack loose to get fifteen.

He packed loose, using two papers to each joint, and got fifteen thin cigarettes for his trouble.

Well, they'd just have to do, that's all. He lit one, carefully, not letting it burn too strong. He inhaled deeply and took a deep breath after it, forcing the smoke down deep into his lungs. He held it there as long as he could, and when he finally exhaled the stream was clear. All air. He felt warm and good. He emptied a pack of Pall Malls, filled it with the reefers and left whistling.

There was no place he could go. He knew the boys would be waiting for him at Wendy's but he wasn't about to go there with his pocketful of hash and nothing for them. If Shank was right, Kenny and Bobo weren't gassed with him in the first place. If they caught him holding out, they might just decide to tear him apart and elect a new mayor.

No, he wasn't about to make that scene. Instead, he just prowled, grinning at people and talking to ugly girls, feeling warmer and looser and easier all the time.

On the sixth smoke, he was really there, beginning to see faces without bodies and bodies without faces. Then he remembered about the redhead. It was about ten o'clock and it took him another half-hour to remember where she lived and to find his way through the suddenly unfamiliar streets.

When he got to her building, he stood looking up at it, watching it curve and waver before him, grinning and thinking: Baby, baby, get ready because Tony Score is coming up for a bite.

He rang the buzzer and the male voice answered. "Yes?"

"Frig you!" Tony said, angrily. He jammed the buzzer and kept his finger there until he heard footsteps coming down the stairs. Then he split to the back. It seemed he was floating when he chinned himself up to the first level, he didn't even feel the steps under him as he climbed to the third floor.

The bedroom light was on and through the undraped sliver of window, he could see that he had picked the right time. The girl was there, lying on the bed, dressed only in a transparently thin negligee. Her breasts bulged out like giant pink teardrops capped with huge dark-red tips of nipple. She turned from profile to face the window for a moment and he could see the rough edges of the nipple rims; they were easily two inches across.

He wanted to open the window and jump in on her, but right then the boyfriend—mean narrow face, tough looking wiry body—dressed in slacks and rolled-sleeved white shirt came in.

"He was gone," he said to the girl.

"Do you think he'll come back?"

"Probably not. But there was a policeman on the corner and I told him to look around."

"Thank you," the girl smiled.

Nuts to you, Tony thought.

The boyfriend seemed more inclined this time. He reached out and embraced the girl, covering her mouth with his while his hand slipped between the folds of the negligee and worked up, catching her breast in his hand and giving a gentle, loving squeeze.

Take a bite, Tony urged as he watched the man's fingers pull at the nipple, bringing it to life. It was the size of a pencil.

Hands locked about her lover's neck, the girl pulled him down with her until they lay side by side, his mouth on her neck.

Down, down, down, Tony thought.

The man obeyed. His mouth went to her shoulders, kissing quietly then to the swell of her breasts where he lavished a hundred tiny nips, his hand coming up to catch a nipple between thumb and forefinger and pluck easily.

Tony felt himself getting hot all over. He lit a new smoke from the butt of the last, inhaled and held it and the world began to swirl before his eyes. He puffed again, one hand rubbing on his pants as the man's mouth went to the extended nipple and closed on it.

Man! Tony thought, dizzily, the image fading and returning as he stared. Man, I'm gonna get me some of that before I go nuts. He stood up, wavering and groped for the window ledge.

"Hey you!" shouted a voice. "Come on down from there."

Tony turned slowly, smiling as if he had just heard the sweetest voice in the world and saw a thick-set spade cop standing in the courtyard, peering up at him.

"Shove it, nigger!" Tony yelled, beaming.

The cop started up the fire escape before Tony could close his mouth. He giggled. "Stupid spade," he said, groping again for the window, squatting down to check the progress of his friends.

The man had his mouth covering the girl's nipple and was nuzzling greedily, murmuring.

Tony tried the window. It was locked. Then he heard the heavy footsteps on the metal stairs, suddenly very loud.

He looked down and saw the cop on the level below him. Whirling, he pulled himself up the next two steps, and clattered to the roof. He stumbled over the ledge, tripped and felt gravel cut into the palms of his hands as he landed. But even the pain seemed remote and faintly pleasant. He got up and ran, the skyline of rooftops seeming to spread out around him forever.

He reached the other side just as the cop clambered over the far edge and heard the footsteps crunching on the gravel behind him. He looked about but there was no adjoining roof; only a sheer drop to the pavement four floors below.

He giggled. Man, that stupid spade thinks he's got me now, he thought. He don't know I can fly.

The cop was within inches of Tony when he saw the boy get up on the ledge, spread his arms and jump.

I'm flying, man, he thought giddily. "I'm flying!" he yelled.

But of course he wasn't.

Chapter 5

Laura Cameron was curled up on the bed, her head tucked into the crook of an arm, her long red hair spread over a pillow. Her eyes were closed.

"It's all taken care of," Jack was saying. "They scraped the boy off the pavement and threw him out with the garbage. You don't have to worry about him, honey."

"I'll still worry," she said.

"But not about him."

"About someone else, then. I hate this neighborhood, Jack. I don't think I'll ever feel safe here."

He sat down on the edge of the bed and she rolled over onto her back, clasped her hands together behind the back of her neck. Stay with me, she thought. Stay with me tonight, sleep with me, hold me close all night long.

She was still wearing the negligee and nothing else. The policeman had wanted to talk with her but Jack had convinced him that the shock would be too much for her. So the cop settled for a word or two with Jack instead. Jack had a way with cops. He was so obviously upstanding, so genuinely moral. Nothing was hidden, either. When you looked at him you decided instantly that he was a good, decent young man from an upper-middle-class family with a degree from a good college and a room-for-advancement job with a respectable firm. Which was precisely what he was.

"You're beautiful," he said.

Her red lips curled in a smile. "I wish we were married," she said.

"Soon."

"Now, I wish. I wish I was your wife and you were my husband and we were ready to bed down for the night. Is that a shameless wish, Jack?"

"Very shameless."

He leaned over, found her mouth with his. At first she simply received the kiss; then, hungrily, she wrapped her arms around him and drew him down to her. She gave herself up to it, taking pleasure from the kiss, giving pleasure in return.

An image flowed into her mind—the kid, the delivery boy, sitting on the fire escape and looking at them, watching Jack handle her body, kiss her breasts. She shivered at the thought.

"I know," he whispered, reading her mind. "Don't be afraid, honey. He's not here now."

He had read her mind, but he had read it wrong. She was not afraid at all. The image of the boy on the fire escape, eyes seeing all, did not inspire fear. It excited her. It made her passionate, for some hellish reason, made her whole body burn with desire.

She kissed Jack feverishly, her hands moving in a frenzy across his back. She pulled him down on her and felt his chest against her breasts. She wanted him to take his shirt off so that she could feel his hairy chest against the tips of her breasts. That always made her wild. Her breasts were huge—they had begun growing when she was eleven, and they had grown like fleshy weeds.

And they were as sensitive as they were large. If he touched them, just brushed them with one idle hand, it was enough to make her blood boil.

"Hey," he said. "Hot, aren't we?"

"Mmmmmm."

"We'll be married soon, baby."

"Not soon enough."

"Three months. That's pretty soon. We have to wait until then, honey. I wish we didn't have to, but it's the only way. It would be like opening a Christmas present at Thanksgiving if we didn't save it for the wedding night."

Not exactly, she thought. Because, to extend the simile, there would be more presents on Christmas. She had an inexhaustible supply of presents, and she would be glad to give them to him forever. But he was right. They had to wait—not because it made any difference on earth to her, but because it did to him. If he slept with her before they were married, he wouldn't marry her. It was that simple. Jack worked that way—he would no more conceive of marrying a girl he had slept with than Barry Goldwater would conceive of voting for Norman Thomas. He was not built that way.

If he could keep his hands off her, that would be something else again. If they waited for the wedding without agitating one another's gonads she might have been able to stand it. But that wasn't how it went. Jack had a moral code that might have been considered absurd in any other civilization but that of twentieth century America. A simple one, really. You could do anything in the world before you were married, except for one thing.

You couldn't have sexual intercourse.

So they petted, ostensibly to a climax. But, she thought, kissing him, it was strictly a one-way deal. They petted to *his* climax. She didn't get one that way. She got hotter than molten lead but she didn't cross the bridge, and each session only left her ready to climb the walls.

He said: "Laura—"

He said it throatily, and she knew what it meant. It meant that the delivery boy was dead and gone, that they were alone, and that in an hour or so he would have to go home to his parents' house and go to sleep for the night. It meant he wanted to have a little sexual fun until then. He managed to get an incredible amount of meaning into two throaty syllables.

"Laura—"

He rolled over, lay on his side facing her. His hand touched her thigh and squeezed. His hands were soft, gentle—he didn't dig ditches for a living, didn't know what a callus was. She wondered fleetingly what the delivery boy's hands were like. Rough and harsh and horny, she decided.

The hand moved. It came up along her thigh, slipped under the negligee, glided over her slightly rounded belly. She felt his forefinger dip momentarily into her navel, teasing her. Then the hand continued its upward climb, moving toward her montizorous breasts.

Yes, she thought. Yes, that's the idea, touch them, handle them, yes, yes—

His hand found her breast. No mean trick, she thought. With breasts the size of hers, it was tough to miss them. If you were in the same room with Laura Cameron, and if you extended a hand, it was an odds-on proposition that you were going to come into contact with a breast.

But Christ what it did to her!

She moaned, a husky moan that tore from somewhere deep in her throat. She wrapped her own hands over his hand and pressed it tight against her breast, feeling the nipple go rigid and dig into his palm. His thumb and forefinger wrapped themselves around the hard bud, pinching, tugging. She thought she was going to go out of her mind.

With his other hand he lifted the negligee, pushed it up until it was all bunched up around her neck. She pulled it over her head, threw it onto the floor. Then she flung herself back on the bed and he leaned over her, each hand trying to surround a breast. He worked on them rhythmically, flexing his hands and relaxing them, and she began to twist on the bed. She couldn't stand it, it was too much, he couldn't work her up like that and then leave her high and dry.

She was supposed to stay that way for three months.

"Your breasts are perfect," he whispered. "Perfect. The most perfect breasts in the world."

His mouth moved down and he began to kiss one breast, the way he had done when the boy had been out on the fire escape watching them. *Your breasts are perfect.* How would the delivery boy have put it? He'd have chosen different words, she decided. Something like: *Honey, you got the wildest pair in the world.* Something along those lines.

A hand moved down to her thigh, then upward along the inside of the thigh. Perfectly controlled fingers that were very careful not to examine too thoroughly, careful not to destroy the delicate membrane that made her an acceptable marriage partner for Mrs. Lacey's little boy Jack.

Oh—

His mouth went on pleasuring her breasts and his hand went on tantalizing her. But his other hand was busy; he was using it to undress himself. He opened his shirt a button at a time, took it off. He got out of his pants, kicked off his shoes. He got rid of his underwear and he was as naked as she was, except that he was still wearing a pair of argyle socks. There was something hopelessly ludicrous about a man making love with his socks on. She tried her best not to think about it.

He was naked. She looked at him, and her hand went out to touch him, to hold him. Now, Jack, now! To hell with getting married, to hell with being your blushing virginal bride . . .

But he didn't.

He pushed her down on the bed. He moved over her, and for a moment she thought he was finally going to forget all about his silly moral code, cockeyed as it was. But he was getting ready for something else. His hands were holding her, one on each huge breast, pressing the two globes of flesh together.

And he began to move.

It was driving her crazy. She tossed on the bed like a whale trying to dislodge a harpoon. Her breasts were ripe with passion, and every movement he made sent her higher and higher in a sexual tailspin. She kissed him wildly, her tongue stabbing at him. She felt his passion mounting higher and higher, felt him climbing rapidly toward the peak.

Then he was there. He shuddered violently with the full force of his climax . . .

Later, when it was time for him to go, she did not walk him to the door. She lay in bed, the sheet pulled up over her, while he dressed and prepared to go. He came to her, kissed her lightly upon the lips.

"Sleep tight," he said.

She tried to follow his instructions. She got tight, but she didn't sleep. Once he was gone she got up and got dressed and raided the liquor cabinet. There was half a fifth of Chivas Regal left and she poured a lot of it over ice and worked on it, hoping the Scotch would put out the fire inside her. It didn't, of course.

She went through most of the Chivas, pouring it on the ice and drinking it down. She was too keyed up for the liquor to knock her on her ear, but it loosened her up a little and stopped her body from trembling too violently. She set down her empty glass finally and stood up. With her hands she cupped her own big breasts, hefting them, feeling their weight.

Damn you, she thought. Damn you, Jack Lacey. All he wanted was her breasts, she decided. That's what he was marrying her for, the bourgeois bastard. She ought to cut them off and mail them to him. Wrap them up nice, put them in a box, enclose a card saying Do Not Open Until Christmas. They were all he gave a damn about.

She shook her head. Actually, it was incredible that she had managed to remain a virgin long enough to meet Jack Lacey in the first place. It wasn't that she hadn't had offers. In high school, all a girl had to do was possess average-sized breasts and she was deemed highly desirable by every boy with two hands. When she was built like Laura Cameron, with a pair twice the size of any other pair at Port Chester High, she got grabbed at three times daily. Boys would brush up against her in the cafeteria. Boys would let a hand wander in the rush through the halls between classes. Boys would, in short, cop a feel whenever given the opportunity.

She'd had her share—more than her share, even—of dates. She had had her share of backseat necking sessions and movie-balcony necking sessions and night-on-the-beach necking sessions. She had necked with one hell of a lot of boys, they had all fondled her breasts with varying degrees of skill, and she had always enjoyed it.

But she had never given in. They would have been glad to change her status from Virgin to Woman, but she was never willing to go all the way. That, she thought, was something to be reserved for Mr. Right.

So she met Mr. Right. His name was Jack Lacey, his father was richer than God, he was a nice guy who treated her well and got her hotter than Chicago after Mrs. O'Leary's cow did her little two-step routine. He was perfect, except for one glaring and fundamental fault.

He was perfectly willing to drive her out of her mind, perfectly willing to handle her and fondle her and kiss her and titillate her and all. But the payoff, the finale, was strictly out of bounds for the time being. And what really bugged her was the way he put up a tremendously unselfish front over the whole thing. He acted as if he was denying himself something, suffering great physical and emotional pain in order to guarantee her purity.

He wasn't the pained one. He always managed to finish, while she always was ready to take a walk along the ceiling when he left her and went home. Unselfish? The bustard had all his fun, and she got nowhere except frustrated.

She got the bottle back and poured the rest of the Chivas into her glass. There was no ice left in the glass but she didn't particularly care. She poured the Scotch down her throat and hiccupped when it hit bottom.

She was sick of it. And she knew she wasn't going to be able to sleep, not for the time being. The obvious ploy was to go for a walk, get some of it out of her system. Walk in that neighborhood? No, thanks. The delivery boy was dead, but there must be a few more like him still breathing, and she didn't want to meet them. It was bad enough living in the neighborhood now. She would be damned if she'd walk around in it at night.

She left her apartment, walked down the stairs and out the door to the street. The night was cold and crisp, and there was a wicked wind blowing. She stood on the curb for less than a minute before an empty cab cruised by. She hailed it and the driver stopped for her.

"Greenwich Village," she said.

The driver turned around, a pained expression on his face. "Lady," he said, "try and narrow it down a little, will you?"

She looked blank.

"That's a big place, Greenwich Village. You got any place in particular you want to go?"

"Some place lively," she said.

"Lively?"

"That's right."

The driver scratched his head. "There's two kinds a places," he said. "You can drink liquor, or you can drink coffee. You want a bar or a coffee house?"

Any more liquor and she would start to spin like a top. She told him coffee sounded right.

"There's this beatnik place," he said. "They sing folk music and read poems and they all smell. They don't shave or comb their hair, anyway. I suppose they smell. I never got close enough to find out."

"It sounds wonderful," she said.

"Great," the cabby said. "Away we go."

She relaxed while he piloted the taxi, heading downtown and west. She decided that she liked the cabby. He hadn't stared at her breasts, not for a second. And he had every right to. She was wearing the canary yellow sweater, and it was a little small for her to begin with and her breasts practically went through it. So she decided that she liked him very much.

She leaned over, squinting at the card with his name on it. His name was Mordecai Schwerner. Wonderful, she thought. And I'm Queen Esther. God, am I high!

She sat back in the cab. Involuntarily, her hands began to roam over her body. She gave her breasts a squeeze, then put one hand under her skirt.

Stop that, she told herself sternly. That's nasty. It makes little girls insane and it gives you pimples . . .

"Lady," the cabby said suddenly, "we're here."

She took a five dollar bill from her purse and gave it to him, then got out of the cab. The wind was stronger now. It chilled her to the bone.

She started to walk toward a sign that said Cafe Desperation. "Lady," the cabby called, "you got change coming."

"Keep it."

"The meter's eighty-five cents and you gave me a five, lady. You sure you don't want some change?"

She walked away without answering him. A tall, thin boy with a dark brown beard was playing doorman, she let him show her inside and point her to a table. She walked to it, sat down in an extraordinarily uncomfortable chair and looked around the place. It was, she decided, a hole.

A rather interesting hole, all things considered. The Cafe Desperation was furnished like a dank cave, with a small stage deep in the bowels of it. A blue spotlight illuminated the stage. On it, a wild-eyed young man was reading poetry to the accompaniment of a piano trio. On the floor of the nightclub waitresses wearing mesh leotards and bulky black sweaters scurried from table to table taking orders. One of them brought Laura a menu. She studied it thoughtfully.

"Coffee," she said finally.

"What kind? Espresso, cappuccino, Viennese, royale, American, mocha?"

"What's the best?"

"Like it depends," the waitress said. "It depends what your particular kick is, like."

She ordered a cup of American coffee and a piece of French pastry. She looked around the room. The audience seemed to be equally divided between Madison Avenue types and beatniks. The Madison Avenue types didn't hold her attention, but the beatniks were rather appealing. She saw a tall Negro boy, his head shaved, with a single golden earring on one ear. He had his arm around a hollow-eyed brunette with chalky skin, and his hand was brushing her breast idly. She saw a bearded man in an Eisenhower jacket, dirt caked under his fingernails. He was drinking cherry-flavored cough syrup with codeine in it.

A real den of iniquity, she thought. Great.

The waitress brought her the pastry and the coffee. On the stage the poet was swinging his arms and shouting at the audience, his unamplified voice easily filling the room. He was saying:

Swine! Pigs! Guttersnipes!
Deep in the holy bowels of hell
The fingers reach for us. Help!
Help us one and all—the horny hands
Scream a hundred curses at the moon
And pluck the testes of the hungry night
Devouring all they touch . . .

She stopped listening to him. Swinging, she thought. I'm just another beatnik, that's all I am. She took a bite of her eclair. It was stale, and the custard filling tasted slightly rancid. She sipped the coffee, which was too strong. She took a cigarette from her purse and lighted it.

She laughed suddenly, trying to imagine Jack at a place like Cafe Desperation. Jack wasn't exactly the beatnik type. Then she looked at one of the bearded boys and tried to imagine him playing with her breasts but being unwilling to steal her virginity. It was equally ridiculous. If she wanted to quit playing vestal virgin, this was the obvious place to pick up a playmate.

The coffee wasn't too bad. She sipped more of it, dragged on her cigarette. A playmate, she thought. A goddamned beatnik playmate. The more she thought about it, the more she began to squirm around in her seat. Damn Jack, anyway—she was so frustrated her groin hurt, so tense she couldn't help twitching like a plucked banjo string.

I'm a banjo string, she thought. Somebody pluck me, huh?

She finished the coffee and stood up. She walked down the aisle toward the stage, weaving only slightly, eyes scanning table after table. She saw a man sitting alone—not a man, really; only a boy with a beard, maybe twenty or twenty-one. She looked at him. He was smoking a cigarette and reading a small book of what was probably poetry.

All right, she thought.

She walked to his table, took a chair beside him. He glanced up, eyes veiled, then returned to the book. She did not move. Then, suddenly, he looked up again. His eyes went immediately to her breasts and stayed there.

"I saw 'em right away," he said. "But like I didn't believe, you know? I looked away, and I saw 'em in my mind, and wow! Like I was a bottle baby, you dig, and I was deprived. Now I'm depraved on account of I was deprived."

He seemed to be talking to her breasts. "Hello," she said.

But his eyes stayed on the montizorous mounds of flesh. He was exciting her with his eyes. She felt her flesh warming although he hadn't laid a finger on her, felt her nipples going stiff.

"Like I've got this mammary fixation," the bearded boy said. "I've got a big thing for breast-flesh, you dig, and it turns me on all over the lot. But you are equipped, baby. You are well-constructed.

You are obviously a mirage in the desert. If I ever told my analyst about you he would fold."

He was crazy, she thought. But he was making sense to her, so that meant that she was crazy too. Well, why not? Wasn't it better to be crazy and get a big kick out of things than to be sane like Jack and go through life wearing horse blinders and shit-colored glasses?

Sure it was.

She looked at the beatnik. "I'm real," she said.

"Are those real?"

"Like yes." It didn't sound right, exactly, but she was trying. Evidently there were times when you used like and times when you didn't. She'd learn, sooner or later. The beatnik didn't seem to notice anything wrong.

"Who are you, baby?"

"Laura."

"Solid. You an exchange student from Kew Gardens? You a little amateur hippy coming down to turn onto boss kicks without getting your feet wet? Or are you real?"

"I'm real," she said. "Like I told you, like."

That sounded better. She was getting the hang of it.

"You dig Ginsberg, Laura? You dig Corso, like? You groove with Ferlinghetti?"

She didn't know who Ginsberg or Corso were, and the other one sounded like something you ordered in an Italian restaurant. Shell macaroni, maybe.

"I dig them," she said. "They're like solid."

"Wow," the beatnik said.

She didn't know exactly how to react to wow, so she didn't say anything.

"You dig this poet up here, baby?"

She looked up, listened to the poet. He was saying:

Shut up, you bitch! Your eyes are black
And your thighs scream at me. Shut up!
Life is a lousy drag, and all the doors
Have turned to Windows. Move out! Give me room!
I'm a tornado, streaking through Kansas, madder than hell,
Going to carry you off to the Land of Oz—

Was she supposed to like him or not? If she liked him and the beatnik hated him, he would think she was stupid. If she hated him and the beatnik liked him, he would think she had more perception than he did. If they agreed, of course, there was no problem.

"He doesn't move me," she said.

"You don't dig him?"

"Like he's not saying a thing," she said.

"Wow! Crazy, Laura girl. Let's split, like. Let's make another scene. Let's fall up to my pad, Laura girl."

"Like let's, like," she said. She stood up and followed the bearded kid out of Cafe Desperation. The poet was shrieking something unintelligible now but she didn't care. She hadn't paid for her coffee and eclair, but she didn't care about that either. And nobody else seemed to care either.

The beatnik, who said his name was Joel, lived in a smelly room on Houston Street. They walked up four flights of creaking stairs to get to it, and when they got there it was hardly worth the effort. There was no bed, just a mattress on the floor. There were no chairs. Joel sat down on the mattress and she sat down next to him.

"You'll dig this," he said, pulling out a book of poems. "It cuts that garbage in Desperation. Listen, like."

She listened, like, while he read her something every bit as unintelligible as the garbage in Cafe Desperation. If there was one thing she did not want, it was poetry.

If there was one thing she did want, it was to get resoundingly deflowered.

Like.

They would get there eventually, she knew. But she didn't want to waste time. She was ready to go already and she had the feeling that if she waited too long the Chivas would wear off and the hotness would wear off and she would change her mind. That would never do. She searched her mind, trying to figure out a properly beat approach. Then she remembered something she had read somewhere.

She took off her sweater and her bra.

That, evidently, was the right approach. Because Joel fumbled the book of poems, dropped it to the floor and stared happily at her breasts. His hands went out, found them, held them, and she began to tremble uncontrollably. Here we go, she thought. Here we go. Stop the world I want to get off.

Joel didn't waste time. He didn't even stop to say *like* or *wow* or anything. Instead he grabbed onto a breast with one hand, and put his lips to the other breast, and stuffed a hand up under her skirt. He pushed her back down on the mattress and began to work on her and she started squirming like a cut-up earthworm. He was nuzzling one huge nipple, his beard was tickling her breast, it was wonderful.

But he didn't stop. He wasn't a silly fink like Jack, not by a long shot. He threw her skirt up around her waist, he tore his own clothing off and scattered it all over the room. He leaned over her and started toying with her again.

And she discovered something. Jack, God bless him, wasn't such a big man at all.

So to hell with Jack.

He didn't take her immediately. He waited, teasing her, touching her, letting her get progressively more excited. Then, when she thought she would simply explode in another second, he touched her . . .

The pain was something she hadn't quite counted on. It was overwhelming, for a minute she thought she was going to die from it. But the pain ebbed and vanished, and then there was no pain at all, only wave after wave of pleasure. The waves came closer and closer together, faster and faster, and each wave was higher than the one before it, and they pitched her up higher and higher and higher.

Joel's mouth was fastened to her breast, his hands gripping her buttocks, holding her. The impact of his body made her shudder all over, made her tremble, was driving her out of her mind. The waves were going way over her head now. They were covering her, drowning her.

More—

And then the peak. Finally, after all the frustration with Jack, after all the times of almost-but-never-quite-there, the peak.

It was perfect.

The whole world ran away and left her alone. She was transfixed, out of time and out of space. The bomb exploded, and after the explosion there was nothing but peace.

They made it a few more times that night. In between they drank sour red wine and he read some lousy poems to her. He was a bore, all things considered, and she didn't figure to be around when he woke up in the morning.

But she didn't figure to be back at her own apartment either. This was the way to do it, by God. Get a pad in the Village, learn the language, and take someone else every night of the week. Just keep on—that was the way. It was the greatest thing in the world, and she wanted all she could get, and the hell with Jack Lacey.

She sighed. She took the book from Joel and tossed it aside. She took the gallon of wine and spilled it all over her body from her neck to her knees.

"Drink me," she said . . .

Chapter 6

They left his place at one-thirty the next afternoon, and at two-thirty he returned alone. He let the downstairs door slam on the bright daylight, struggled up the four flights of stairs trying not to think about them, or the rancid darkness, or the stale hung and hungover smell of his room. He was entirely unsuccessful. The stairs winded him, the darkness depressed him and the odor of his rat's nest curdled his stomach.

He closed the door, used the knob for a hook for his clothes and dropped onto the bare mattress, naked and exhausted. He shielded his eyes with his forearm, although there was no light coming in, only a glaring sun behind his eyes, and he thought:

Now I lay me down to rest

After playing with a chick with a great big breast

Swinging, he thought. Grooves. Probably one of the best things he had ever written. He really should get up and write it down before he forgot it. He always got his best ideas in bed. Like boffing Miss Balloon-Breasts last night. And this morning. And early this afternoon.

Christ, he had ridden like one of the four horsemen of the Apocalypse. Or better yet, one of the four horsemen of Notre Dame. The Maker of the Virgin Laura.

That had been a surprise. A first. She had been saving it just for him. Growing it, protecting it, fondling it, keeping it new and shiny as she strutted around her youth in Kew Gardens or wherever at the same time that he was growing out in Barnesville, Nebraska. She had waited, impatiently, while he practiced up on a farmer's daughter here and a town whore there, waiting until Destiny or Fate or The Great Lecher decided it was time to throw them together, to impale her on the point of his passion. Whammo! And that's the way a virginity ends, not with a whimper but a bang.

Not bad, he thought. He really should get up and write all this down. He was letting an entire slim little volume of bad poetry slip by him. *Selections After Sex* by Joel Richard Kelton. The reviewer in the *Times* would write:

Mr. Kelton's work, although generally genitally centered, conveys the driving force of the sex act itself. Far from seeming like a first effort, his verse bespeaks a wide experience in all types of fornication and hints at an admirable maturity of perversions . . .

Not so many, Joel thought. There was Judy who would not take off her clothes and swim bare with him when they were twelve but who was more than glad to strip down to swim—or anything else—when they were sixteen. There was Alma who did it for love for anybody; and Connie who only did it for love if you didn't have the money. There was Ruth who always insisted on undressing in the bathroom first (maybe she had some other guy in there, he'd thought). And then there was Nancy, and Rosalie, and Wanda—good Barnesville girls all, flowers of the prairie, whores of the wheatland. They had all been charmed by his long talks and impressed by his other endowments . . .

Ah, but you couldn't spend your life in square old Nebraska, no matter how good the crops were. Not if you were bright and perceptive anyway, not if you had something important to tell the world, not if you were the country's great unsung poet.

Joel Kelton, Poet Laureate. The-poet-Laura-ate. Ha. Sure, he was a poet. Give me a blank john wall and I'll write you a poem.

Author! Author! Take off your pants and take a bow. Thank you, Thank you. And for my next trick . . .

Myrna.

Myrna, the talking Myna Bird, who had more of a beard than he had at the time. Myrna, his first New York Nookie, in whose black mystery he discovered the black mystery of the Village: expresso and bad poetry and cheap wine. Ah Love! A loaf of stale bread, a gallon of cheap wine, a book of bad verse and thou. Myrna, beneath the stairwell in Barrow Street. Ah *what* Wilderness!

"The wilderness beneath her dress

"Is tamer now and wilder less."

Oh, Jesus, he was going out of his mind!

He dug his fists into his eyes and rubbed them red, rolled over and pressed his face against the rotten tufts of the mattress. He had to get some sleep; he could feel his body turning numb on him. He couldn't stay up all night and make love then go all the next day without sleeping . . . like he was some nineteen years old or something. Hell, he was twenty-four. A rather gaunt and undernourished twenty-four, granted—but twenty-four nevertheless. He should have the blood of tigers coursing through his veins, the good healthy robust blood of the Nebraska farmer, his father, who could get up at five and plant ten acres by noon.

But he didn't have it. He felt dull and sluggish, with a congested ache in his groin. And after only planting one virgin, too. He had sown only a few seeds and would reap no harvest. Or would he? Maybe Laura Large-Lungs would bear him an heir, suckle his child to her breast. Christ, what a healthy kid that would be! King Kong, maybe. King Kong Kelton.

"Ladies and gentlemen, you have all heard of the seven wonders of the world. But now I am about to show you the eighth wonder. From far-off Africa, the Dark Continent, to your amazement and astonishment, I now show you the greatest beast of all time . . . King . . . Kong!"

Oh, wow. He had to stop visiting Murray and staying up 'til two o'clock watching those old movies. He had to start eating some decent food, too. And cut out drinking and smoking so much. And lay off the virgins. And stand up straight when he walked. Joel, eat your spinach . . . and leave that girl alone!

Yes, tomorrow he would start leading the Good Life. Clean up this hole a little, give the library back some of their books. Hell, maybe some other people would like to read Hart Crane too. You can't be selfish. Spread the wealth around. But wasn't that just what he was doing too much of?

"Don't spread the manure too thick, Joel-boy," his father always said. "Makes it bad for the crops."

But Joel-boy hadn't listened. Joel-boy had slung crap around until his arms ached . . . and his legs . . . and everything else. He had ploughed high and wide and handsome. It was a kick for a minute, then crap for a long time afterward.

Well, tomorrow he'd change. Tomorrow he'd get started on that big poem. The biggest. The Mommy of All Poems. A

Decameron! A Laura Cameron! A great big sprawling boob of a poem.

Yeah, tomorrow. But right now he had to get some sleep.

He slept. It was eight-thirty at night when he awoke, and he lay in the darkness, looking at the luminous face of the travel alarm until nine. He had to get up and get something to eat. Hunger was starting to gnaw away at the lining of his stomach, to eat down into his bowels. But he was so comfortable lying immobile that he let the extra torturous half hour click away.

Finally, he got up. His body felt coated, a shower would be very much in order. Wrapping a towel around his waist he padded out into the hall, wincing with disgust as his bare foot crushed in on the shell of an already-dead roach. The bathroom door was open part-way so he did not bother to knock; the light was on so he did not have to pull the cord. And, he thought in the same chain of logic, the shower was going so he did not have to bother to turn the spigots. How nice, he thought groggily, tossed the towel on the john seat, pulled back the curtain and stepped into the stall.

Naturally, somebody was in there. Of course, it was a girl.

Her name was Candy—at least that was what Ben, the artist whom she lived with, always called her. She was twenty, twenty-one and very pleasant to look at—at the moment anyway. She had black hair that reached down to her waist. She wore it plaited in a single braid when she was dressed. Right then, it hung down like a curtain, making the pert little rounds of her buttocks look even saucier. She had good long legs and—as she turned now to face him—Joel saw she had nice perky little breasts, milk white up to the ridge of red-brown nipple, and capped with soft little-finger size tips of dark red flesh. Joel soaked that all in—and the rest of her—as the shower water began to soak him.

"Hi," Candy said. "You in a hurry?"

Joel shook his head.

She looked at him. Her gaze started at his face and then dropped, using the point of his beard as a plumb line, down his rib-thin chest and below. She seemed to like what she saw, for she smiled.

Joel smiled back. Without thinking about it, her body had worked its magic on his body, playing the Hindu snake-charmer . . .

Aching though I am, he thought, stiff as I may be, I would like nothing better than to sample some of this Candy. But he didn't. He didn't make a move toward her. Instead, grinning sheepishly, he backed out of the shower. He wrapped the towel around his waist and sat down on the john seat to wait for her to finish. It was a simple matter of courtesy, the code of the Village. She was Ben's chick and he was Ben's friend. So if they were going to make it together, she would have to be the one to make the move. He couldn't; he wouldn't. First of all, Ben was six-four and weighed in at about two-forty; second, she didn't really turn him on that much at other times because she didn't have the brains of a really smart roach; third, if you live in a place then you obey its code—moral, immoral or amoral—otherwise you move out.

The code didn't apply to outside chicks, of course. Anyone who came down to Village—like Laura—was fair game. Unless she was living with you regularly, any stud could try to push her over at any time.

But Candy was labeled and he wouldn't even try to rub up

against her. She would have to do the rubbing; and that, in its way, would signify that she was finished with Ben and on the open market again.

So he waited, wondering if she would try to give him a play and doubting it. Ben had enough to keep her happy, he knew; and even though Ben was even less of an artist than he was a poet, Candy didn't know the difference between a Picasso and a *Saturday Evening Post* cover.

When she emerged five minutes later, he found out how right he had been.

"It's all yours," she said, reaching for her towel.

"Thanks," Joel said.

"Lemme just dry off a little first, huh?"

"Sure."

He waited while she dried off. She did it in a manner cultivated to tease. But he watched nevertheless.

First she started to shake herself, putting her hands on her hips and swinging her torso, making her breasts bob like tight pendulums. Then she began to handle them, dabbing at the nipples with the towel, rubbing them with gentle circling strokes. Next the towel went behind her and she wriggled her back dry against it. Then, of course, as the piece de resistance (a piece with great resistance, Joel thought) the towel went between her legs. Grinning lewdly she worked the cloth like a saw, back and forth, back and forth.

Finally she was finished. She wrapped the towel around her waist, bundled a second one into her wet hair. Her rosy breasts still bare and now pointing straight, she stepped out of the stall as he stepped in.

"There we go," she said.

Joel turned on the water and pulled the curtain.

"Hey," he heard her call above the shower.

He poked his head out. "What?"

"You had dinner yet?"

"No."

"You wanna eat with me and Ben? We're having spaghetti for a change. There's plenty." Her hand went to her left breast and she pulled abstractly at the nipple, aiming it at him.

"No thanks," Joel said. "But say hello to Ben for me."

"Yeah, I will. See you."

"Groovy," Joel said.

He regretted his decision an hour later. After showering and giving the beard a careful inspection for lice, he dressed and discovered he was tapped.

The realization did not actually surprise him. He remembered having ten dollars on him the night before, ten dollars which was ear-marked almost to the penny for his meals until the check from his father arrived in two days. Although he could not account for the money, he had lost more than ten in the liquor-and-expresso haze of coffee shop nights. He did not bother to check in another pair of pants or his second jacket. At best, he might come up with an odd quarter which, added to nothing, would still not buy him the meal his stomach was craving.

Goddammit! he thought, mildly. Goddamn this rotten room that costs eight bucks a week. Goddamn stupid farmers like my father who charge too much for their stinking vegetables. Goddamn those greedy bastard restaurant owners. Goddamn everybody who has conspired to leave me hungry now. In short, he thought, goddamn the whole world except for Joel Richard Kelton, who is responsible for tossing away his last ten bucks.

And now what, poet? Whither goest?

He knew he could go to Ben to bum a buck, but chances were that Ben didn't have a spare buck. Since he had never borrowed from him before, he liked the idea of preserving his well-to-do status.

The Rockefeller of Houston Street, he thought. Yeah, that was he, all right.

So he would go to Murray and get himself a meal, and pay for it by sitting around for three hours while Murray psychoanalyzed him, dissected his id and his ego. After they were both half in the bag, Murray would come down to the same old bit that he only went for females so much because he was really a latent homosexual and trying to cover it up.

Well, it was better to be a fat contented queer than a starving straight poet, so he'd trade that garbage for some eats. If only Murray was home . . .

Murray was home. But he was just leaving. He answered the door with his Homburg and his cane in his hand, his face creased with obvious annoyance at a caller this late. But he brightened considerably when he saw it was Joel.

"Ah, the budding Whitman. I didn't expect you this evening. Did we have an appointment?"

"No. I'm just hungry."

Murray's fat forehead wrinkled with dismay. "I'm so sorry. But my cupboard is bare and I was just leaving."

"How about loaning me a deuce until doomsday?" Joel said. "I really am hung."

"Of course, of course," Murray said, withdrawing his billfold. "Only too glad to be of assistance. A patron of the arts. Oh—" He looked abashed and spread the empty billfold before him. "I'm afraid I'm temporarily embarrassed," he said. "Financially impotent, as they say."

"Groovy," said Joel. "Just give me a can I can crawl into then."

"You do look rather peaked," Murray said. "But then you are naturally sallow-skinned, in addition to suffering the physical ravages of—shall we call it—over-indulgence?"

"I don't dig you," Joel said. "I haven't seen a chick for days. Weeks. Maybe even months. I'm strictly priest-material, man."

Murray smiled appreciatively. "You lie with great charm which is almost better than telling the truth. However, the truth in this case happens to be that I was at the Desperation last night and I saw you with a young lady who, even to my rather jaded eyes, was constructed along fairly remarkable proportions. She was, as you might put it, 'top heavy.'"

"She was pretty breathy, wasn't she?" Joel said.

"Indeed," said Murray. "And no doubt as comfortable as she appeared. You must tell me about it sometime. Naturally, it only confirms what I've told you many times. An obvious return to a mother-image like that when it's quite plain that you have incestuous feelings toward your father—"

"Bury it, man. I'm too hungry to listen to that now."

"Of course," Murray said. "Well, I'm sorry I can't be of more assistance in your hour of need but, as I mentioned, I'm just on my way to an engagement. Ah!" He snapped his fingers. "*Die antwort!*"

"What?"

"The answer. German, my boy. You shall come with me. I'm going to a party where there will be food galore. Not only are you most welcome, I'm certain, as the host is a very close friend of mine, but you can feed yourself to your heart's content."

"Whose pad?"

"Whose place?" Murray said. "Is that your question?"

"Check."

"Oh, it's not so important. I doubt if you've ever heard of the man. He is renown for his generosity, and I can guarantee you a luxurious spread as well as an abundance of beverages. But come, we must leave immediately. I'm late now and it's a goodly trip to Brooklyn Heights."

"Forget it," Joel said. "Riding in those holes in the ground drag me. Like, I'd rather starve, man."

"Nonsense," Murray said, hooking his arm onto Joel's. "We shall hail a taxi, of course. Come."

Joel regarded him oddly. "Like how you gonna spring for a hack, man, when you're tapped, too?"

"Details, details," Murray said impatiently. "I told you that our host is a most generous man. I have no doubt he will come to our aid at the moment of crisis. Come, let us be gone."

It was a twenty-five minute ride to Brooklyn Heights. During it, Murray avoided any further questions about the party and concentrated on getting Joel to discuss his "liaison" with Laura. Joel had expected that. Murray, an admitted homosexual of the non-proselyting sort, had a insatiable interest in Joel's conquests of—what he termed—"the unfair sex." He disguised his curiosity to some degree by saying that it was necessary for him to know a great deal about Joel's background activities if he was to judge his poetry with any critical faculty.

Murray taught English at a Bronx high school and regarded himself as a representative literary reaction to Joel's poems. They had met one night at the Desperation where Murray cruised regularly searching for intellectual young men of promise and/or easy virtue. He and Joel had come to intellectual-but-not-physical terms at the start and on that basis their friendship had grown. Joel tolerated it because Murray was usually good for a meal and a drink and he enjoyed the older man's apparently genuine interest in his work.

"That incident," Murray said when Joel concluded the tale of Laura's defloration, "will be of no material use to you whatsoever in your work. But, of course, you realize that."

"Dig," Joel said. "But why?"

"Because it was so blatantly synthetic. You wanted to possess her for all the wrong reasons, mostly because she was so incredibly overdeveloped. And she in turn was yielding, obviously, because of a hurt suffered at the hands of some other man. It was a match of misdirected passions from the outset. And that explains why you suffered the self-abnegation this afternoon when you parted."

"Who said anything about self-abnegation?" Joel asked. "I grooved. The chick was a ball in bed. She was as phony as a rubber cork but she was real in the hay so what's the problem?"

"Joel, Joel," Murray said wearily. "You are still so young, so naive. You really have no idea of the value of true passion and the meaning of a genuine physical attraction."

"But you do," Joel said sourly.

"You refuse to understand," Murray said. "I am not going to

press the point further. Let's let the conversation drop. I believe we're almost at our destination anyway. Yes, we are. The second house on the left, driver."

"Right." The cab stopped and the hack threw the flag. "It reads two-sixty," he said over his shoulder.

"So it does," said Murray. "And there shall be a dollar tip in it for you, my man, if you will be kind enough to wait a mere moment. Joel," he said, getting out, "I think the gentleman would prefer that you remain here while I go in and find our generous host. It may allay his fears that we are trying to beat him out of his just recompense."

"Dig," Joel said.

"What'd the fat guy say?" the driver asked.

"Cool it," Joel said. "Just don't listen to him."

Murray returned a minute later in the company of a short, silver-haired man who wore a red dinner jacket over striped tuxedo pants and a butterscotch yellow ascot. He was at least fifty, perhaps as much as ten years older. But Joel found it difficult to tell because his soft square face was heavily powdered and his cheeks were pinked by rouge. He fixed Joel with bright, electric blue eyes as Murray made the introductions.

"Randolph, this is Joel Kelton, a young poet. Joel, Mr. Randolph Deering, your host."

"Groovy," Joel said, taking the extended hand and receiving a soft moist squeeze for his trouble.

"My pleasure," Randolph Deering said. "Please call me Randy. All my dear friends do."

"You can call me *pishka* if you'll pay this fare," the cabbie said. "I ain't ready to retire yet, you know."

"Oh yes," Murray said. "Randolph, this is most embarrassing for me but it seems—"

"I understand," Deering said. He produced a billfold patterned with tiny fleur-de-lis, withdrew a five and handed it to the driver. "No change, thank you," he smiled. "And sorry to put you to any trouble."

"Any time," the cabbie said, rubbing the bill. "You sure you don't want me to wait?"

"I don't think that will be necessary," Deering said. "Thank you." He turned to Joel: "Shall we go in?" He put his arm around Joel's waist as they started toward the door. "I know there are many people here who would be enchanted to meet you. A poet! Oh, we must have a long quiet talk before the evening is over. Murray knows all the most interesting people. How I envy him his mobility."

Murray beamed.

All the people who were enchanted to meet Joel were queer. In fact, everyone inside the large high-ceilinged ornately-decorated living room of the Deering house was homosexual, and Joel figured that included the two stunning dark-haired long-legged girls in black leotards who acted as waitresses.

Some, he was surprised to note, were even queerer than Deering. There was one little man with shoulder-length blond hair and gold curled-toe slippers who sat on the window seat plucking a lyre; there was a husky, football-player type who wore mascara, lipstick and a single diamond earring; there were two skeletal-thin old men with gray crewcuts, pipes and leather-elbowed jackets who sat holding hands on one of the long sofas; there was a short, roly-poly Madison Avenue looking homosexual with curly hair, a Brooks Brothers suit and woman's spiked heels.

A flower garden, Joel thought. A goddamn pansy patch.

But there was also food. Two long tables of it: platters of canapes, a glazed ham, sliced turkey, strips of corned beef, roast beef, pink slabs of tongue, potato salad, pickles, sauerkraut—the makings of a great feast. And all of it untouched. The "men" walked by it, carrying drinks in their hands, crossing to exchange conversation-partners, forming and re-forming in intimate whispering little groups, laughing, talking, some singing but no one stopped to sample the food.

No one but Joel. As soon as Deering disengaged himself, he made a beeline for the table. Without caring if anyone was watching or not, he began to load a plate with both hands, trying one of everything and two of most things, wolfing the food down while he reached for more, washing it down with gulps of martinis from the trays the leotard girls were circulating.

"I see you're enjoying yourself," Deering said, his hand on Joel's waist.

Joel nodded, his mouth full.

Deering smiled. "Good. I was almost tempted not to put out any food tonight because I know, by past experience, that my friends never touch a bite. They really have poor appetites, poor souls. It's good to see someone who enjoys eating."

Joel gave him the look he deserved; but Deering's expression was bland and innocent.

"I'll see you later," he promised, with a squeeze. "I must set up the projector now. Do find yourself a good seat. I'm afraid there aren't enough chairs."

And he was gone.

Murray came over. "Well, it didn't take you very long to find the viands, I see."

His mouth still full, Joel gestured him to try some.

"Perhaps just a bit of caviar," Murray said. "I am on a diet." He chose a canape with care and swallowed it whole.

"Hey," Joel said, wiping his mouth, "what's the flick?"

"Flick?" Murray said. "I don't believe I understand."

"The silver screen," Joel said. "The cinema. The movie, square."

"Oh, oh," Murray smiled. "You mean you don't know? Oh, then this will be a treat for you. I'm afraid Randolph has the same old films which I've seen a dozen times, but I'll be able to enjoy them now just by watching your expression. Come, let's find a good seat."

"Well, what is it?" Joel said. "Let me in on the bit."

"You'll see," Murray said, as they sat down on the couch closest to where Deering and the tall football player type were unrolling a movie screen.

As soon as the first frame flickered on the screen, Joel saw. They were stag movies—for homosexuals, of course.

What else? he thought, feeling foolish for not having expected it. But even with that fact established, the films were different from anything he had anticipated. They had no titles and no plot at all. Each opened in the same way with a full length shot of a man undressing, then moved across what was probably a very cheap hotel room to a second man who began to undress. Both were very tall, strong virile types with hair bristling on their chests and muscles that rippled as they, rather purposefully, flexed while stripping. When both were naked, they crawled onto the bed from opposite sides and, with no delay, began to kiss, embrace and fondle each other.

The camera work, Joel noted, was unimaginative throughout. It did not vary in the least, remaining a static front view shot of the figures on the bed during each of the five films.

The second differed from the first only in that the background was a little more elegant, the bedroom of an apparently expensive private home. But the actions and the physical attributes of the actors were the same as they were in the third film and the fourth (with the slight difference that in the fourth film, a third participant entered into the writhing tangle of limbs and torsos).

Judging by the reaction of the audience—who were prone to loud obscene comments and jokes which evidently involved men who were present but which Joel did not understand, as well as a series of vulgar groans and liquid noises—the fifth film was the best. The action seemed identical to the other four, but the background was the confines of a bathroom; and the intimate antics of the two men were interrupted by the sudden appearance of a third man from behind the shower curtain.

Joel just stared dumbly, taking frequent sips from the pitcher of martinis which he had found at his feet.

When a fourth man appeared from behind the curtain and joined in with the other three, the audience was convulsed with laughter. Just like the clown car in the circus, Joel thought.

It was then he realized just how drunk he was. He turned to say something to Murray, and saw that Murray was not there. In his place was the short man with the shoulder length blond hair who was embracing the roly-poly Madison Avenue man in heels and kissing him passionately.

Joel tried to stand but found his legs too weak. He fell back to the sofa again, bumping into another couple stretched out lengthwise in each other's arms.

He looked around horrified, and in the flickering light of the projector saw that everywhere around him men were in intimate consort with each other, kissing passionately, simulating the activities on the screen.

He stood up, pushed by a man who was hugging another, and looked around the darkness for the doorway. His head spun and the floor looked as if it were about to come up and meet the ceiling.

He weaved, reached out for balance, touched a bare back and withdrew his hand with disgust.

Suddenly, the beam of the light from the projector snapped out; the screen went dark but the lights did not come on. Instead the whirring click of the film was replaced by the increasing murmurs which seemed to emanate everywhere about him.

He started from the room and tripped over the prostrate form of a man who was breathing heavily, his hands rhythmically stroking another man.

Joel stared at them for a frozen instant, then realized the second man was Murray.

"Murray!" he shouted and tried to wrench his friend up.

"Get away," Murray said viciously. "Get away." He pushed out at Joel, sending him crashing against the food table.

Voices of surprise and anger rose in the darkness.

"What is it?"

"Who is it?"

"What's going on over there?" piped a reedy soprano.

Joel stumbled from the room and found himself in a darkened hallway. He groped for the light switch but found the wall smooth. Moving on, he slid his hand along the wall until he found a door. He turned the handle and entered.

It was not the way out.

It was the entrance to a giant, luxuriously furnished bedroom with walls of carved dark Philippine wood paneled with stained glass and inlaid with tiny dark stones. On the ceiling was a huge gold-framed painting of two bulbous muscled men involved in the act of mutual gratification.

The scene turned Joel's stomach.

Deering was standing there, smiling at him.

"Well, this is a pleasant surprise. I've been looking all over for you."

"Lemme out of here," Joel said.

"Oh no," Deering said. His hand went to the pocket of his red jacket and withdrew holding a small gray pistol. "Oh no," he said. "I wouldn't think of doing that. Why we haven't even started to have our little fun yet."

"No," Joel said. "I don't—"

He stopped when the door opened behind Deering and Murray entered.

"Murray," he said. "This guy's crazy. He's got a gun and he wants to—"

"Everything all right, Randolph?" Murray asked courteously.

"Fine, thank you, Murray. Did Austin give you your money?"

"Yes, thanks. You certain you won't need me for anything else?"

"Not at the moment," Deering said. "Unless, of course, you'd like to watch."

"I'd be delighted," he said.

"Fine. Would you be good enough to hold the gun on Mr. Kelton while I disrobe?"

"Murray—" Joel started.

"No," Murray said. "Please don't say anything. Just get undressed like a good boy."

"Murray—"

The fat man shook his head. "Please, Joel. Just relax. You'll enjoy it much more that way. And think of the wonderful poems you'll be able to write afterward."

"All right," said Deering. "I'm ready." He took the gun from Murray. "Now, Joel dear. Come over here." He smiled warmly.

Chapter 7

The high school was a post-war building in Parkchester, which in turn was a moderately fancy name for a not-that-fancy section of the East Bronx. It was three stories high, made of brick and concrete and equipped, foolishly, with picture windows. The architect had evidently known little about high school students and less about the East Bronx; a surface familiarity with either would have ruled out the use of picture windows from the onset. After three-fourths of the windows had been shattered by the charming natives, wiser heads prevailed. The picture windows remained. They were now protected by close-knit metal screens which saved them from everything but an occasional stray bullet.

Murray Messner stood in the front of a classroom on the second floor. He was dressed quietly—a gray business suit, a plain white shirt, a dark and somber tie. The Homburg and the ebony cane were back at his apartment on Charles Street. He stood at the blackboard chalk in hand, looking like nothing more or less than a fat little man crowding middle age, finishing an unexciting life as an English teacher in—God help us—the New York City public school system.

"I saw the bust of Oliver Cromwell walking through Westminster Abbey," Murray said. "This is an example of improper usage known as a dangling participle. Obviously, the bust of

Oliver Cromwell was not walking through Westminster Abbey. So, unless the speaker had been smoking the wrong variety of cigarettes—"

The class tittered appreciatively. Murray Messner, he thought sourly, Classroom Comedian. It wasn't easy to win the admiration of a gang of apprentice hoodlums. All you had to do was intimate a surface familiarity with vice in its myriad forms and they took you for a brother.

"We can see that it is the speaker who was walking through Westminster Abbey, the I in the sentence. The construction is an improper one. One might better phrase it *While walking through Westminster Abbey, I saw the bust of Oliver Cromwell.* Or, perhaps, *I saw the bust of Oliver Cromwell while I was walking through Westminster Abbey.* Or—"

The bell rang. With a display of heretofore magnificently concealed energy, the class leaped to its collective feet and scurried into the hallway.

The last class of the day for Murray Messner. There was one hour remaining before school ended, but it was an hour he could spend alone. He might go to the teachers' lounge to smoke a cigarette—the teachers smoked only in the lounge, just as the students smoked only in the lavatory. The distinction—a minor one—was that the teachers were allowed to smoke in the lounge, whereas the students were not allowed to smoke at all. An extraordinarily minor distinction, and one hardly worthy of mention.

He didn't feel like smoking in the lounge, or like sitting in the lounge without smoking. Or, in short, like going to the lounge at all. He walked slowly to the window, propped his arms up on the ledge and stood gazing out through the steel mesh at the Bronx.

The window afforded him an excellent view of a housing project, tall and gleaming, with an unredeemed slum flanking it to the right. He looked alternately at slum and project and tried to force himself to relax.

I saw the bust of Oliver Cromwell walking through Westminster Abbey.

I saw the bust of Murray Messner going down Cranberry Street in Brooklyn Heights.

Or—

He turned from the window, paced back and forth along the tiled floor. He walked in back of his oak desk and dropped heavily into the wooden chair behind it. He took a cigarette from the desk drawer, picked up a pack of matches. Teachers were not supposed to smoke in their rooms. He lit the cigarette, inhaled, blew out smoke.

Hey, teach, he told himself. Teach, you are a first-class SOB.

He smoked. True enough, he thought. True enough. He earned fifty-three hundred dollars a year, before taxes, and he spent sixty-five hundred dollars a year. He made up the difference by pimping for an old faggot. He thought about the party the night before, remembered the way Joel shuddered with disgust while Randolph took his pleasure with him.

Not quite cricket, he thought. Bad enough to round up the navy and the marines for old Randy. Far worse to sell your friends to him.

Now take hold of yourself, he told himself sternly. In the first place, young Joel is no creature of virtue. He's an unkempt little stallion who dirties the sheets with the blood of virgins, and his life is not sufficiently moral to warrant recriminations over his betrayal. Even if he didn't enjoy Randy's attentions, they wouldn't make him leap into a bath and slash his wrists. Very little would make Joel leap into a bathtub, as far as that went. Unless there was a big-breasted wench in the tub.

Hell, he thought unpleasantly, Joel wasn't even a friend as far as that went. The pathetic poet sponged off him shamelessly, ate his food, drank his liquor and gave him drivelly doggerel to read and admire. One doesn't exploit friends, perhaps, but one could exploit Joel without a guilty conscience.

He heard footsteps in the hallway. Quick as a bug he hopped to his feet and scuttled to the window. He opened it, flipped the cigarette out between the screening, closed it again. He went back to his desk, breathing heavily. A rank coward, he thought. Eight years at the foul school and scared of a smoking violation. A coward.

Back to Joel. You're all wrong, he told himself now. In the first place Joel *was* a friend. He would not be one again, not after the delightful debacle of the previous evening. But he had been one. True, Joel had mooched from him. True, Joel had consumed liquor and food and had borrowed small and non-returnable sums of money. But the relationship had been a symbiotic one. If Joel fed on him, he in turn fed on Joel. He listened to Joel's stories of sexual prowess with the unfair sex—identifying with Joel? Identifying with the woman? Deriving some vicarious compensation for his own heterosexual inadequacy? Oh hell—whatever it was, he had listened and enjoyed it all. They had stolen fun from one another, had taken each from each something necessary. And he had betrayed their friendship.

Then take the matter of Joel's virtue, or lack thereof. He could not accuse Joel of being amoral. As a homosexual, he could certainly avoid thinking in conventional moral terms. Joel took girls to bed for mutual pleasure, and his personal moral code permitted this. His personal moral code did not permit him to take men to bed—which was what Murray had gotten him involved in. No matter how he looked at it, he had sold out a friend. He was in the final analysis just what he had presumed himself to be. He was a first-class SOB.

He wanted another cigarette. Go ahead, he thought. Take one out, scratch a match, light it. You can't use your lighter. It's at home, it never goes to school with you because on the back it says "To Murray from Randolph." Innocent enough taken by itself; but beneath the inscription was the indecent crest which Randy had designed for himself. No, the lighter had to remain at home.

But matches serve the same purpose. Go ahead—light up, smoke, and get ready to throw the cigarette away as soon as some obnoxious student passes in the hallway. Go ahead, fool.

He did not light the cigarette. He remained at his desk, nervous and uncomfortable, until the bell rang. There were no after-school meetings, nothing to waste still more of his not-that-precious time upon. He got his coat, put it on, left the school and took the subway home.

Home was a first-floor garden apartment on Charles Street, an expensive and comfortable apartment in a quiet and comfortable brownstone on one of the Village's best streets. He walked inside, closed his door, sank into a deep leather chair. Home, he thought. A faggot's home is his castle. Relax, Murray Messner.

He smoked a cigarette, using Randy's gift lighter this time and placing the cigarette in a long ebony holder. When the cigarette was gone he stubbed it neatly in a sterling silver ashtray and pried the butt from the holder with his fingertips. He stood up, walked to the record player. He took a Bartok string quartet from the record holder, was in the act of placing it upon the spindle when he changed his mind. He slipped the Bartok back in its jacket, walked to his tape recorder and threw a switch.

He was seated once more in the leather chair when the tape began. He listened.

Like nothing in the world, Murray baby. I met this broad in the San Remo, dig, and I was standing at the bar working on a beer when she hits one. A married broad, like. Maybe thirty, I don't know. Big ring on her finger, Saks Fifth on her back. Older than me, but who cared? Built, Murray.

You're so transparent, Joel. Such an emphasis upon breasts, such an interest in older women.

It's so oedipal, Joel.

Oedipus, schmoedipus, as long as he loves his mother. Man, like I took her up to my pad, you dig? I finished my beer and she was giving me the hip-to-hip jazz and I just like reached over and grabbed a handful of bozoom. That did it for her. Away we go to my pad, and five minutes later I'm in like Flynn. You should have been there, Murray baby.

I'm sure I should have. You've come a long way from Nebraska, Joel.

Is that supposed to be a dig? If it is you're not reaching me.

Not a dig.

You want to hear more, Murray?

Certainly.

Solid. So we get finished balling, like, and I figure it's back to her old man and the bourgeois world. But not for this chick. She gives me this coy smile and says she's got an idea. I ask what she got like on her mind. She grins, cute as a flea.

Cute as a pubic louse, you mean.

Say, like that's not bad, Murray. Cute as a crab.

But this was some broad, man . . .

He turned off the tape recorder. A unique perversion, he thought, and one that would no doubt rankle young Joel since the budding poet had no idea he'd been taping their little discussions. Buy why in the world *had* he been taping them?

A good question. You, he told himself, are a sick man. You ought to get your skull checked out, ought to spend some time on a couch telling all to a sympathetically Freudian ear. He'd gone the analysis route of course, spent two months in therapy with a Park Avenue broad who seemed like a dyke to him. All he'd gotten from the sessions were a monumental bill he was still paying off, and a further indoctrination in psychiatric terminology.

Nonsense, he thought. Nonsense and stuff. You aren't a profound neurotic, Murray Messner. You're just a fairy. If you were a man, you'd be a dirty old man. As it stands you're a dirty old queer.

You have champagne tastes and a beer budget. You like expensive clothes and a good apartment, and little props like hat and gloves and cane. You like smoked clams at two bucks a tin and Martell V.S.O.P. at ten dollars a fifth. You like front-row seats to hit shows.

So you are a very moral little faggot. You never seduce anyone. You make a large thing of sleeping only with men who are similarly inclined, you keep away from school children and you live the good life.

But you want that extra money. So you round up beamish boys for Randolph Deering and hold them at gunpoint and watch like a Munro Leaf watchbird while dearie Deering goes a-queering.

God help you, Murray Messner, you fat little faggot. God help you . . .

He had grown up on West 76th Street in Manhattan, gone to P.S. 93 and Stuyvesant High, been queer ever since the feeble-minded Kraut janitor stole his maidenhead a few weeks after his fourteenth birthday. It was funny now, because he went back to the old neighborhood often enough. It was a gay area now, not the middle-class neighborhood he had grown up in.

He had been queer since that time, in the cellar. That night, alone in bed, he felt guilty about it—not so much because of what precisely had happened but because the janitor was a German. The incident seemed to him to be the ultimate Nazi rape.

But he had enjoyed it. And he continued to practice various forms of homosexual activity from that time onward.

Still, he had tried once.

He remembered the time. He was twenty-six, he had just broken up after a prolonged (three weeks; that was a long time for an affair in the gay world) love affair with a lisping queen named Helen. Helen had thrown him out of his-her apartment, and he walked through the Village with a suitcase in one hand feeling thoroughly ridiculous and wishing that Macdougal Street would open up and swallow him.

It didn't, of course.

So he walked down Macdougal Street, swinging the suitcase,

feeling ridiculous. And he remembered the Kraut janitor and wondered if it had started then or earlier, deep in childhood, maybe tied in with toilet training or some comparably traumatic phenomenon. And it occurred to him that it might just have been one of those especially annoying accidents of fate. Maybe he had not been destined to be a homosexual at all. Maybe he was as normal as the next person—he looked to his right at that particular moment, and the next person turned out to be a broad-shouldered dyke with her arm around a frail blonde femme. Jarring. But maybe he was normal—a latent heterosexual, to coin a phrase.

Well, why not?

He stopped at the Remo for a drink. He started to order a Grasshopper, then changed his mind. Let's be manly, he thought. Let's have something a little gutsier than a Grasshopper.

So he ordered a straight shot of bourbon, and choked on it.

Outside, nervously smoking a cigarette and still carrying the annoying suitcase, he decided that he had to test this new-found hypothesis of latent heterosexuality. Pick up a girl, give her a play and see how much fun it could be. That, of course, was the mannish thing to do.

A girl?

He was scared to pick up an ordinary girl. In the first place, he wouldn't know what to do. In the second place—well, the first place was enough in itself. Any old girl wouldn't do. He needed professional help.

I.e., a prostitute. A scarlet harlot.

He loaded himself and his suitcase into a taxi and rode to Times Square. He walked over Forty-Second Street to Eighth Avenue, trying his best to ignore the pitch from the male prostitutes congregated in front of Bickford's. He didn't mince, his cheeks weren't rouged—how did they *know* he was gay? Well, the devil take them. Maybe he wasn't gay after all. Maybe he was straight. He would have to find out.

The third bar he tried, a darkish ginmill on Eighth between Forty-fourth and Forty-fifth, yielded up a bounty of harlots. A few sailors were there, picking up tarts. But fortunately there were enough left over. He let one of them fasten herself on to him. She was Cuban or Puerto Rican, a thin-faced flat-chested wench who confided that her name was Conchita. Why did he pick the flat-chested one? Why didn't he get one with big breasts?

Let's do this in stages, he thought. First a flat one, then a gently rounded one. In time, if all goes well, maybe he could work his way up to a cow.

He took Conchita to a room in a Hell's Kitchen hotel. He paid Conchita twenty dollars. Conchita took off all her clothes and lay down on the bed and he wanted to run out of the room with his tail between his legs. But instead he steeled himself, stripped and joined her on the worn-out bed.

Her body was soft. So, unfortunately, was his.

She tried everything. She squirmed, she touched him, and she imprisoned his hand and rubbed her warm genitals against his cold fingers. Nothing seemed to stir him. Until in desperation he closed his eyes and stroked Conchita's soft buttocks, and in his mind's eye she changed from girl to boy. Then it was easier. When he was using her as the Kraut janitor had used him in that lousy basement room, passion began to move him and build within him, it became good. The girl shivered and writhed, and it got better. Finally he pitched face forward, straining to catch his breath.

I did it, he told himself. I did it, I made love to a woman, I did it. I am a man!

But of course he wasn't.

Memories. He got up from the chair, stirred not so much by memories of Conchita as by those that followed it. Memories of his return to the shady groves of fagdom, memories of men and boys. Memories.

He showered, washing himself with slightly scented soap. He dried and dressed. The workday business suit stayed in the closet, safe and sound until it was time to return to Parkchester and play regular-guy-Messner again. He put on a Lou Magram shirt, a pair of pearl-gray flannel slacks, a powder blue sport jacket. He added cashmere socks and Italian loafers. He set the Homburg on his head and picked up the ebony walking-stick.

Prowling clothes, he thought. Cruising clothes. Here we go, off on a manhunt. Correction, please. A faghunt. A queerhunt. A pansyhunt.

He tried the Purple Grotto on Eighth Street. Nothing at all was doing there. He passed the time of night with a few old friends, listened to a Sinatra record on the jukebox, and left. He passed a Pam-Pam and decided he was hungry. The Pam-Pam would combine food with cruising. It was a gay restaurant, part of a chain of gay restaurants that blanketed New York. If you were sufficiently determined, he thought, you could live a lifetime in New York without ever seeing anybody who wasn't as queer as an oblong watermelon.

The Pam-Pam yielded no prospects. He had the chef's salad

with Roquefort, liver and onions au maricon, and a slab of apple pie with cheddar. He finished up with coffee, left the hip-swiveling waiter a good tip and went out to make the rounds again.

In Danny's Den, he scored.

He went into the place, a cellar club located subterraneously on Bank Street, and gave the place a quick once-over. No one interesting seemed to be present, but he could afford to kill time over a drink. He took a table alone and ordered a whiskey sour. He sipped it, played more Sinatra records on the juke box, and waited.

Then the sailor came by.

The sailor did not look gay. But sailors rarely did look gay, and sailors often were. All those weeks at sea without a woman around, it could get to a man. So could other sailors. And sooner or later someone would start a game of Drop the Soap, and homosexuality would make another convert.

The sailor didn't look gay, then. But he looked like fun. A huge, strapping youth not more than twenty-five at the outside, with a narrow waist, broad shoulders and a face that looked as though it had been hewn from granite—and by a primitive artist at that. Not Grandma Moses though. It wasn't that sort of face at all.

He took a breath, ready to stand and make his play. But that wasn't necessary. Amazingly enough, the sailor walked directly to his table, looked him up and down, and took a seat across from him.

"Hiya," the sailor said.

"Hello," Murray said.

"Just got off the damn ship," the sailor said. "Came down to the Village, figured I'd find me a little excitement. This looks like a pretty exciting place."

"It is."

"You come here a lotta the time?"

"I come now and then."

"Yeah." The waiter had arrived. "Double shot of dark rum, huh? Straight, no chaser."

Ah, Murray thought. A man's man.

"Only thing is," the sailor said, "I gotta few days of liberty coming and I got no place to park. I hate like hell to sleep at the ship and I can't shell out five bucks a night for a stinking flop in a stinking hotel. I figured maybe I could find a place to stay for a couple of days."

Ah, Murray thought. Ah, you have come to the right place, dear boy. I could always take you to Randy, of course. Randy would be highly pleased with you. He likes rough trade. He'd pay a few hundred dollars to me and all I'd have to do would be to deliver you.

But I won't do that, dear. I won't sell your sweet body for a mess of potage, not today.

I'll save you for myself.

"You could stay at my apartment," Murray said.

"Yeah?"

"Surely."

"Well, that sounds pretty good. Matter of fact, that's sort of what I had in mind."

Murray beamed.

"We could go there now," the sailor said. "Soon as I get that rum down me. That waiter takes his sweet time, don't he? The wormy bastard."

The waiter appeared, double-shot of rum in hand. The sailor tossed it off neatly and put the glass down empty. He stood up. Murray put bills on the table to pay for his sour and the sailor's rum. He stood up and they walked out of the bar. His apartment on Charles Street was only a few blocks away, and they covered the distance quickly. He opened the door and the sailor followed him inside.

"Nice place you got here," the sailor said.

"I'm glad you like it."

"You must make a lot of dough."

He shrugged.

"That picture," the sailor asked, "What's that?"

It was a Picasso etching. He told the man this, and he nodded thoughtfully.

"A real Picasso?"

"That's right."

"Cost a lot?"

"It's only an etching," he said. "It cost about a hundred fifty dollars."

"Yeah?" The sailor walked to the wall and lifted the framed etching from its hook. "This Picasso," he said. "He a queer?"

"I don't think so."

"But he could be," the sailor said. "Right?"

"Well—"

"Sure," the sailor said. "What the hell, he might be. The whole goddamn world's fulla queers. Place is swimming in queers, for God's sake. Hell."

"Wait," Murray said.

"Goddamn queers," the sailor said. He slapped the framed etching over his knee, shattering the glass. He tore it free of the frame and ripped the paper to shreds. Murray watched helplessly. What on earth was happening? What was going on? What was *wrong* with this man?

He said: "Please—"

But the sailor wasn't listening. He had picked up a blue vase from the oblong table and was holding it at arm's length, staring at it.

"What's this?"

"It's Wedgwood. Listen—"

"Wedgwood. He queer too? Oh, the hell with it!"

The sailor threw the vase at the fireplace. It sailed lazily through the air like a soft pass on a football field. It struck the brick fireplace and shattered completely. Murray stared at the pieces and bits of broken china. The man was a lunatic.

"I want you to leave my home," he managed. "I want you to get out, I want you to go away, I want you to leave me alone. I want—"

"I thought I was staying here tonight, buddy."

"That was a mistake. I want—"

"You know," the sailor said, "I bet you thought I was queer. Didn't you?"

"You approached me," Murray said. "You came to me. I didn't come to you."

"You thought I was queer. Right?"

"I thought—"

"You thought I was a goddamn pansy. You thought I was some

kind of a fruit. You want to know something, buddy? There's one thing I can't stand, it's a goddamn queer. I like women, you got that? I *hate* queers. You know what I think is a real kick? I think beating up a queer is a kick. Taking some fruit and pounding the living crap out of him, that's a kick. I think I might just do that now."

"Please—"

"Then I'll get the hell out of here." He was advancing on Murray now. Murray backed away, backed into a corner and cowered there. The sailor moved closer.

"Then I'll get the hell out of here," the sailor went on. "I'll find myself a woman, you got that? I'll take that broad and put it to her until she sees stars. I'll love the daylights out of her, you goddamn queer. But first I'm going to work myself up knocking the crap out of you."

Murray said: "No."

The word had very little effect upon the sailor. He balled up a hand into a fist the size of Gibraltar and pushed it easily into Murray's face. Murray felt something break in his nose. Blood washed over his upper lip.

"This next one's in the mouth," the sailor said. "That oughta put you outta commission for awhile, huh? Your friends won't go near you, you goddamn queer."

Murray tried to dodge the punch. He didn't manage it. He felt a tooth break and felt his head bang horribly against the wall. Oh, Christ, he thought. This idiot is going to kill me. This maniac is going to murder me.

"Am I gonna love up that broad," the sailor said. "Am I ever gonna make that broad see stars!"

He slammed a fist into Murray's stomach. Murray sagged, began to fall in slow motion to the floor. A foot came up hard and fast, sailed between his thighs, caught him flush in the groin.

He screamed.

"You scream like a goddamn broad," the sailor said. "I'm ruining you, huh? By the time I get through nobody'll have any use for you."

Another vicious kick in the groin knocked Murray unconscious. He didn't feel the rest of the beating at all.

Chapter 8

Andy Garino's fist hurt. He touched the knuckles of his right hand tenderly as he strode down Charles Street. The bones felt numb and dully aching but it was a pleasant ache, satisfying. He touched something wet and sticky. Blood, he thought.

Whose blood? His or the queer's?

He felt again and found a split in the skin by the side of the knuckle. The blood was just beginning to congeal.

Both their bloods, probably. His *and* the queer's, mingling together right now. What could you get from the blood of a queer? He wondered. Clap? Syph? Rabies? Maybe it could make *you* queer. He didn't know. Lawton would know, though. Lawton would be able to tell him exactly what it would do to him and what you had to do for it. Lawton had probably beaten the hell out of more goddamn queers than any man alive. But Lawton wasn't around then. He was busy laying up with some fat blonde pig who was—not too surprisingly—the first woman they'd met when they left the ship. Lawton, that bustard, his best friend, had walked away with the first pig he saw, leaving him alone on his first liberty.

Well, the hell with Lawton. He could manage by himself. Crap, there were only three things you were supposed to do on a liberty. Get drunk, shack up with a broad and beat the hell out of a queer. Lawton had told him that himself. Well, he had a good start on number one, already taken care of number three and that only left number two to be accounted for.

But first he'd better wash off his hand or put iodine on it or something.

He took care of that in the next bar he came to. It was a greenly glowing hole three steps below street level. He ordered his double rum from the barman as he walked back into the head.

He thought to himself: There better not be another queer in there because I'll just have to let him go.

There wasn't. The head was barely big enough for him, just a closet with a sink, a john, a roll of toilet paper and two dispensers on the wall. He washed his hand, rubbing it with the gritty soap until the skin began to whiten and then let the water run over it for a minute. He shook it dry while he looked around for some medication. One of the machines sold condoms. It was labelled FOR THE PREVENTION OF DISEASE ONLY.

Sure, Andy thought. Nobody did it just for the hell of it anymore. They did it just to protect each other from a dose. Well a bag wouldn't be much help for his hand unless he wanted to wear it like a glove. The idea made him grin. Lawton would like that. He'd get a big laugh out of that idea. If Lawton was around, he'd do it. He'd cram his fists into two bags and when they'd find themselves a broad. Lawton would say something like: "Look sister, can you help us out? My pal here put his hands someplace where they shouldn't have been and now he's got these stuck on 'em. We never seen any of these before but you look like the kind of lady who knows what they're all about. How about helping us out?"

Andy grinned again. Hell, he wished Lawton was here. This goddamn liberty was gonna be crappy alone.

The other dispenser sold combs. Only ten cents. Well he had a comb but he could always use another. He fumbled in his tight pants, got out a dime, inserted it, turned the crank. A bright red plastic comb scraped down the chute. It was imprinted Otto's Place in gold letters.

That was nice, Andy thought. His first souvenir of New York. Something to send to his girl, if he had a girl. He should wrap it up and mail it to Margie with a note like:

When you're finished using this, why don't you shove it and let your new boyfriend have fun looking for it.

That dirty whore!

There was no mirror in the head, but using the shiny tiled wall as a reflection he ran the comb through his wavy black hair, spending a great deal of care on the front. There was not very much to care for.

Christ, he thought. Three lousy months in the Navy and all he had to show for it was calluses on his hands and no hair on his head. And, oh yeah, a chipped tooth where that bustard Matson had sent his fist flying. That son of a she-dog. If Lawton hadn't stepped in and brained him with a bucket, Matson probably would have knocked the living crap out of him. Why the hell hadn't he hit back? Why the hell didn't he duck in the first place? He saw that punch coming from a mile off.

Because he was yellow, that's why. He was yellow and scared pea-green. Ah, it was only his second week in the Navy. What could you expect? He was just shy, that's all. Hell, he wasn't yellow, he'd fight when he had to. Sure. Hadn't he just kicked the crap out of that queer? Right. And it had been a real kick, too, hadn't it?

No.

He had felt lousy when he was doing it and he felt even lousier now. Then why? Because you were supposed to, that's why. Because that was Navy, sonny. Rough, tough and ugly. Because the whole goddamn fleet was just a bunch of crap-heads, that's why.

Oh shove it, Garino! You just need some more booze in your gut and a broad twitching under you. Well, number one and number two, here we come.

He jammed the comb in his back pocket and pushed out of the head. His drink was waiting for him at the end of the bar. He slapped a buck down, downed the rum in two swallows and snapped his fingers for another one. Then he looked around to see who had noticed him.

It appeared that no one had. Otto's Place was almost empty. A pair of ditch-diggers were at the other end of the bar, nursing beers and watching some pig in tights and a top hat dancing her tail off on the TV; the barman was listening to some hen-pecked looking crumb crying into his Scotch; all of the booths were empty except the last one. A lone woman was sitting there, staring into her drink. The green glow of a rotating Schlitz sign made her look wrinkled and about two hundred years old.

Andy looked away, sipped his new drink. When he looked back, the Schlitz globe had rotated to white and he saw that the woman was not more than thirty, clear-complexioned and not bad looking. Her hair was a light brown, brushed up in—what at the start of the evening might have been called—a high class *bouffant,* like a beehive. Her features were sharp, high cheeks, narrow chin; she wore a plain black dress with a single strand of pearls that had some class to them. Andy thought she might be a society broad who had been slumming, got too potted and was left behind by her party.

On second thought he decided she was probably a hooker in her last good dress and too stoned to give a crap about her hair. Society broad, hell, he told himself. Lawton would get a kick out of that idea ("Who'd you think she was, kid? Princess Grace?" And then he'd roar out that gravel laugh.)

Well, princess or just alley cat, she still had the right equipment and he was gonna take it out on a shake-down cruise. He ran his new comb through his hair, picked up his drink and swaggered over to her booth.

"Hey," he grinned. "Just got off the damn ship. Came down here, figured I'd find me a little excitement. Is this a pretty lively place?"

The woman didn't look up from her drink nor give any sign that she was aware of his presence.

"Looks like you're almost dry there," Andy said. "Here, lemme buy you another." He whistled at the barman. "Two more here, bud." He moved closer to the table. "You come here often?" he asked the woman. She didn't answer or move, still staring fixedly at the glass before her.

"Hey," Andy said. He reached out and shook her arm. "I'm talking to you." He smiled widely.

The woman looked up. Her face was chalky white except for the slash of red across her mouth, her eyes looked like large ebony marbles. "Who are you?" she said slowly.

"Andy Garino. Just in off the *Morgan.*" His smile faded as

soon as he heard himself say it. Never give 'em your right name or your ship, Lawton had warned. An angry broad can make more trouble than a deckful of thirty-day wonders. "That is, I used to be off the *Morgan,*" he amended quickly. "I'm with the *Oregon* now." He wondered how the hell he was going to get around to giving himself a new name but at the moment it didn't seem very important. The woman appeared to have received none of his information.

"Who are you?" she asked again.

"I just told you, lady," Andy said. "Andy Garino. Open your ears." He grinned warmly.

The barman brought the drinks.

"My friend seems like she's had a couple," Andy said, paying him.

"Always," the barman said and left.

"You feeling okay?" Andy asked her. "You want me to take you home?"

The woman shook her head. Her hand went to the strand of pearls and she fingered them curiously.

I think I got myself a wacko, Andy thought. "Lady," he said gently. "you all right or what?"

She responded not by looking up but by looking down, seeing the new drink and downing it in a single practiced motion. She shivered slightly, set the glass down and watched the last trickle slide down the inside of the jigger. The Schlitz globe turned to green making her look aged again. "There," she said. "Take me away from here."

"Sure," Andy said. "Sure." He tossed off his drink and stood up. "You got a coat or something?"

She shook her head, stood up and walked out ahead of him. Outside Otto's, she stood facing the street, her back to him.

"Well, where to?" Andy asked jovially. "Hit a couple of spots maybe?"

"Let's go to your place," she said quietly.

"Well, okay," he grinned, sliding his arm around her waist. "That's the way I like to hear you talk. For a minute there, I didn't think you even knew I was around." He squeezed her to him and she moved stiffly. "Now then," he whispered into her ear, "the only little problem we got is that I don't have a place. But that ain't really a big problem, now is it?"

She didn't answer for a moment. Then: "Let's go," she said. "Anywhere."

The neon of the Dorchester Hotel grinned at them from up the street and they headed toward it.

They didn't make it immediately. Passing an alley, her hand suddenly went to his arm and she pulled him into the darkness with her, threw her arms about his neck and forced his mouth to hers in a kiss that was hard and hot.

He was too startled to react until he felt her tongue wedge between his lips and thrash violently, hungrily. Then his hand went to her breasts and he squeezed, cupping them, smoothing at the warm, mobile rounds that rolled and yielded under the light fabrics of dress and bra. Mouths still merged, she pulled him down until they were on their knees in the alley. Then forward onto her. He started to push at her skirt but she anticipated him, pulled it up above her waist, wrenched down her panties.

"Now," she said hoarsely. "Now, now!" And she was already in the motion before he had his pants unbuttoned.

He didn't like the idea of doing it there on the damp cold stone but that objection melted as her bare legs twined about his thighs, her arms held him breathless against her heaving breasts, she writhed and squirmed with a sharp delicious irritation that uncoiled his passion like a wire. They were locked in furious tempo, faster, faster . . .

Twenty minutes later they were in a three-dollar-a-night room at the Dorchester. She had not said another word. He started some embarrassed comment as they picked themselves up from the alley, but that trailed off when he saw that she did not even bother to brush herself off, just stood there facing the street, waiting. Then he kept silent, too, except to tell the desk clerk what they wanted. He signed the register Mr. and Mrs. John Smith, figuring that would get a wink from the man. But the clerk—short, bald, tired-looking—just handed him a key, wearily pointed up and went back to his racing form.

She started to undress before he had the door locked. She kicked off her shoes, unsnapped the clasp on her pearls with one hand, pulled the dress over her head, unhooked her bra, and slipped her panties down her legs. She left the clothes in a pile where they had fallen, crawled onto the bed and closed her eyes.

Andy stared at her in wonder. She was one helluva good looking broad, he thought. Her skin was pure cream, her breasts looked like great scoops of vanilla ice cream topped by thick dark cherries. Her stomach was flat and hard; her thighs were firm and her legs shapely.

He kept his eyes on her as he undressed, folded his uniform neatly and placed it on the single chair, then went to the light switch.

"No," she said as he clicked it off.

He clicked it on.

A real cutie, he thought.

"Okay," he grinned. "I like to see what I'm doing, too."

He lay on the bed beside her and turned.

"Go get a bottle," she said, eyes still closed.

"Sure." His hand closed over her breast and he rubbed the dark nipple with his thumb. "Later."

"Now," she said, rolling over to face the wall. "Now, now." Her voice rose. "Right now! Go get it!"

"Okay," Andy said. "Right now. Take it easy." He shook his head as he stood up. Oh man, I got one this time. I got a genuine wacko. The jackpot. A lush nymph.

There was a phone on the dresser and he clacked the cradle until the desk clerk answered.

"Yeah?"

"Listen, chief. How about sending a bottle of good Scotch up pronto?"

"You kidding, sailor?" the man said. And hung up.

No room service, I guess, Andy thought, and felt foolish.

"Listen, honey," he started.

"Go out and get it," she said, not turning.

"Yeah, in the morning, okay? I got something better than booze right here." He turned off the light, crawled onto the bed and pulled her to him. She was stiff as a board and cold as ice.

"Oh now, come on," he said, rubbing her breasts, his other hand snaking between her thighs.

But she was like a corpse, tense and frozen.

"Okay," he said, "okay." He got dressed in seconds and was

hurrying down the stairs in a minute more. The desk clerk looked up as he passed. Andy gave him a dirty look in return. There was a package store a block away. He ran to it, pushed past a drunk weaving in the doorway and shouted his order to the clerk, peeling off bills.

"Forget the bag," he said. "And the change." He grabbed the bottle and was outside, tearing down the street.

Never leave a broad alone until you're finished with her, Lawton had told him. She'll cut out on you faster than you can say spit. Stupid sonofabitch, he cursed himself. He should have given it to her cold or not, and to hell with the bottle. If she was gone, he thought, taking the stairs two at a time and throwing open the door . . .

She wasn't.

She was lying right where he had left her.

"Here we go," he said, relieved.

She reached her arm languidly behind her. He unscrewed the cap and handed the bottle to her. She rolled off onto her back, tilted the fifth up and let one . . . two . . . three . . . gulps bob her lovely white Adam's apple. A shudder convulsed her entire body, she tilted the fifth up and took another long swallow.

"Easy," Andy said. "Save some for me."

But she was finished then. She held out the bottle to him.

He took it, grinning, determined to top—or at least match—her performance. But on the second swallow he felt his throat starting to flame and he put the bottle down, breathing fumes.

Son of a seacook, this tart can really handle it, he thought admiringly.

"Come on," she said, drawing her knees back and arching her back.

That was enough to turn him on, fast. He tore off his clothes, this time leaving them in a pile beside hers, came to her. They met and merged, lips, chests, stomachs, thighs, passions. Within seconds they were rocking and jerking spasmodically, her nails screaming down his back, his hands digging at her buttocks . . . the thunder of cannons exploded in his ears and the final spasm was an earthquake, a torpedo jarring him to the core and sending trembling wires of sensation racing across every nerve in his body. *Jeez!*

He got to say that four more times in the hours that followed. Each time the earthquake of pleasure-pain that rocked him was better, deeper, more intense; but each time the small voice in his mind that said "Jeez" became weaker and more agonized—until finally it was only a moan from the core of feeling that was as much hell as paradise.

He never knew when night turned to morning. They kept the light on throughout. When he was with her, it was impossible for him to leave her soft grinding ecstasy; when he was not, he was too exhausted to move.

Several times he felt himself drifting off into an aching clouded sleep and was grateful to it for removing him from the temptation of her body, which he could not resist. But each time she awoke him, her mouth—smelling of fresh liquor—licking over his lips, her hands kneading his congested body, her breasts rubbing softly, deliriously against his chest. And when finally all those wiles failed, when he thought he was lost to her until sleep could rejuvenate him, she did other things that whipped his dead passion into life, she kindled the cooling embers into new flame and used him as he lay motionless, squirming—until he reluctantly joined her again and they galloped together on another nerve-tearing race to eternity.

Even when he was paralyzed with weariness, unable to join her, she took her private pleasure at the cost of his agony, drew the last vestiges of his strength from him and left him drained and withered.

Finally, she let him sleep.

She was standing naked before the mirror, running his new red comb through her hair when he awoke.

He opened his sticky eyes, looked at the soft glowing rounds of her buttocks, the reflection of her dark-tipped breasts in the mirror, and felt himself respond in spite of himself. He rolled over on his stomach and tried to smother his passion.

"Good morning," he heard her say.

He mumbled into his pillow, felt the bed sag as she sat down beside him, felt her cold fingers needle his buttocks.

"No," he murmured.

She laughed. "All right." She settled for kissing him, letting her mouth linger enough for him to feel a gentle warm pain.

"You're branded again," she said coyly.

He ignored her.

"What's your name?" she asked.

"Told you last night," he mumbled.

"I thought you probably did but I don't remember.

He muttered something incoherent.

"Artie Reno?" she guessed.

He rolled over to face her. "Yeah," he said.

She beamed at him, looking incredibly fresh and rested.

"Well Artie Reno, we're out of breakfast juice."

"I don't want any breakfast," he said.

"I do. I think the package store on Seventh and Bleecker is open. Why don't you take a little walk down there?"

I don't believe it, he thought. "You want another drink?" he asked incredulously.

"Yes, thank you. Don't you?"

"Sure," he said. "Sure." He stretched, yawned and ached in every muscle.

"How come you're not tattooed?" she asked, running her hand down his chest.

He shrugged. "Never got around to it."

"All sailors are tattooed," she said. "All sailors *have* to be tattooed. I'll tattoo you," she said, pressing her mouth to his abdomen and drew in a long kiss. "I'll tattoo my name on you," she said.

"No."

"All right then, just my first initial." She kissed again. "You're lucky it's only a V," she said. "It could have been an M."

He pushed her away. "No."

"What's the matter, sailor? Can't you take it?"

He stiffened. "I can take it," he said. And he pulled her to him. She came, smiling, her hand squeezing him fiercely. His mouth went to her breast and bit her nipple. Then they were at each other like tigers, clawing, biting, kissing, pinching, until he managed to straddle her, his knees digging into her soft body. She looked up at him with bright defiant eyes, opened her mouth and ran her tongue about the circle of her lips.

That reached him. Like a frog he was off her, then he came at her again with all the fury of his anger and love, and though each movement pained him and tightened the aching chain around him. And smiling that same delicious, aggravating smile, her hands still behind her where he had pinioned them, her breasts raised and pointed, she stared at him with eyes wide with delight at his efforts and his pain.

When he left her, he dressed and went down to get the bottle. He didn't say a word. It wasn't necessary. She had outlasted him in the battle which, traditionally, should have been his supreme victory, the conquest of body and spirit.

But it wasn't the war, he thought, paying the desk man another three dollars for the night that was to come. It wasn't the war at all. He'd play her down to her knees or die trying. Either way, it was going to be one hell of a liberty. Yeoww!

Forgetting about his aches, he bounded out the door of the hotel and hurdled the first hydrant he came to.

"Yeeeowwwww!" he shrieked, frightening bystanders.

What a story this would make for Lawton. For the whole goddamn ship! Whatta broad she was! What a great goddamn beautiful sex-happy broad!

"Yahooooo!" he howled.

She had showered and was lying with a towel draped over her legs when he returned with the fifth.

She smiled up at him and reached out for the bottle.

"All I want now is a nightcap," she said. She took a healthy swallow. "Mmmmm," she wriggled and stretched. "Now I'm going to sleep for awhile, sailor." She tossed the towel to the floor. "And you can look at me and plan some nice surprises for later."

She closed her eyes, smiling like a cat, and cuddled up to the pillow.

He watched her until she was asleep. Just the sight of her nakedness aroused him, but he knew he couldn't possibly be any good at the moment. And besides, he didn't want to wake her.

Let her sleep, he thought. Let her get a good sleep. Jesus, he thought gently, do I love this broad!

He sat there grinning for another half hour, and then he could not bear to have this shoddy little room containing his happiness. He wanted to scream and shout from the roof tops; but he settled for one more coyote bellow when he got outside again.

Now what the hell could he do? It was almost one then, she would be sure to sleep at least four hours, maybe more. He knew he was too keyed up to even think about sacking. So what the hell could he do until five?

He started with four eggs and a double order of bacon at a luncheonette. On the sixth slice of toast, washed down with the fourth cup of coffee, the idea hit him.

Oh Jeez, it was beautiful. It was sensational. It was too goddamn good! He pounded the counter with his fist when he thought of it.

He was going to get himself tattooed.

Of course. Sure. What else? Goddammit, it was perfect! He would have her name tattooed on his chest.

Except that he didn't know her name.

Well, he'd wake her up and ask her. No. That probably wouldn't make her too happy. Christ knows, she had earned a little goddamn sleep. Well, he'd just have her initial tattooed on him then. V. She said her first name started with V. Virginia? Vera?

Verna? Violet? What the hell kind of names started with V? Oh, the hell with it. Just the V would do. A great big goddamn V with a heart around it and a goddamn bushel of flowers underneath. She'd love it! She'd flip!

"Yeeeowww!" he roared and pounded his fists on the counter.

Naturally he didn't know where to find a tattoo parlor. But the newsie at the corner told him there were plenty out at Coney Island. He got subway instructions, squirmed impatiently on the train for thirty minutes, went tearing like a bat out of the station and into the nearest needle emporium.

"Get out your crayons, chief," he shouted at the small, red-headed hunchback sitting in the small room. The walls were covered with pictures of designs and photographs of muscle-bound men proudly displaying their body artwork.

"Siddown," the man said. "Relax. No hurry. Other customers I'm not expecting."

"Get out the pin, mac," Andy said exuberantly. "I'm in a big hurry."

"All right, all right." The man got up, handed Andy a book and then began to assemble his equipment. "Find what you want," he said.

"I know what I want," Andy said.

"You know what you want," said the man. "Everybody knows what he wants. Only most of them don't want tattoos any more. The Health Department knows what they want. In six days, they're closing me down. Did you know that?"

Andy shook his head. "Let's get on with it," he said impatiently.

"Get on with it," the hunchback said sadly. "Forty years I've been here and he wants me to get on with it. You want to know why they're closing me down?" he asked. "I'll tell you. Blood poisoning. Some schlemeil kid gets blood poisoning from some crap artist, so they're closing down all the tattoo places in the city. Some joke, huh? You think that's gonna stop the kids from getting tattooed? No. You know what they'll do? They'll do it themselves with their own dirty needles and ink from a bottle. Then you'll see some blood poisoning."

He inspected his box of needles, chose one and held it up to the light.

"Had a girl in here this morning. Real tough girl but nice looking. Very nice meat all over. She wanted to get tattooed so bad she was almost hysterical. Believe me, if I wasn't here to do it, she would have done it herself. You know what she wanted? Her tough boyfriend got himself killed last week. Jumped off a building or something. Who knows with kids nowadays? So she wanted his name tattooed on her for like a monument. You know where she wanted it?"

The man grinned, and pointed to below his waist. "Sure. His name she wanted from her belly-button in a line straight down."

He grinned again. "I was only too glad to do it for her. But you think she'd get all undressed so it would be a little easy for me? No. Just up with the skirt and pulls her little black panties down just enough. Ach. No pleasure I get from life anymore. So I tattoo his name, Tony. T-o-n-y. And her pants are almost down to where I can see everything. So I say to her, 'Why don't you have his last name put on, too? I won't charge you extra.'"

He shook his head. "Wouldn't do it. Like I'm going to do something to her if I see what she's got. I'm an old man," he said, stretching out his hands. "Maybe a little touch with the finger I give her, what else? But no. Ach. It's a terrible world."

"Yeah," said Andy. "But let's get on with it, huh?"

"Okay, okay. I'm all ready. Now what do you want?"

"A V. On my chest."

"That's nice. Patriotic. Right after the war, I use to get a lot of business like that. But since forty-six, forty-seven, not one. You'd think the boys they come back from Korea, a little honor to the victory. But no. No more flags. No more eagles. Just 'Mother', girls' names and stuff like that, that's all they want. Some country, America."

"Right here," Andy said, baring his chest. "A great big V in a heart with a basket of flowers under it."

"You got it," said the man. "I could do it with my eyes closed." He reached for his inks, then drew back and turned. "You know what I've always wanted to do? My dream? You talk about a V for Victory. I've always wanted to tattoo that on Churchill.

"You know Churchill? The Englishman with the cigar? He's the one that's always going like this with his fingers. V for victory. So I've always wanted to tattoo that on him. I wouldn't even charge him a cent. It would be an honor for me. Like having a picture in a big museum. Ach! So you think when Churchill visited this country, he came to Coney Island so at least I could get a shot at him. Of course not." He shook his head. "What a world, never anything good happens."

"Yeah," Andy said. "But how about it, huh?"

"Okay, okay. A V in a heart with flowers. You got it."

A V in a heart with flowers. And what a V! It was the size of the V that she had between her legs. And even curlier, with little spirals going this way and that way. And the heart encompassed both of Andy's nipples and looked so real you'd think it was going to burst. And the flowers were a whole goddamn garden, almost the width of his stomach.

Jesus, he thought. She was going to *love* it! It was all he could do to contain himself from tearing off his shirt to look at it again on the subway ride back.

It was three-thirty when he arrived at the Christopher Street Station and three-thirty when he dashed up the stairs at the Dorchester.

Then, grinning inanely, he forced himself to stop and knocked, lightly, on their door. No answer. She must be sleeping, he thought. He opened the door gently and peeked in.

The room was empty.

He sprang inside and looked wildly about. Her clothes were gone and the fifth he had bought that morning was lying on the bed. Empty.

Oh Jesus, he thought.

First he tried the bathroom. Empty. Then he raced downstairs and almost assaulted the room clerk, shaking him violently as he asked him When, when, when did she leave? The clerk hadn't noticed.

He was outside like a bull, tearing down the street to Otto's. But she wasn't there and the barman wasn't the same one who had been on duty the night before.

He tried six other bars in the neighborhood before the first wave of anger wore off. At the seventh, he lingered over two shots, letting himself cool down.

He'd find her. He had two more days of liberty left and he'd find her if he had to check every bar and every hotel room in the whole goddamn city.

But even as he thought it, he knew it wasn't true. He'd never find her. And probably by tonight, he'd be too worn out to keep looking. Christ, he didn't even know her first name. V, that's all he knew. Just V. What a laugh the story would give Lawton.

And what about the tattoo?

Oh Jeez!

CHAPTER 9

The guy left at seven-thirty. He left about a third of a quart of Cutty Sark, a half pack of Luckies, and most of his manhood. He also left a crisp twenty dollar bill. Vicki found it on the bedside table under the bottle of Scotch. She took a long drink, looked at the bill again and started to laugh like a ticklish hyena.

The damn fool thought she was a whore! That was one for the books, all right. Imagine Vicki Flagg charging for it, for Christ's sake! Didn't the schmuck know a full-fledged nympho when he had one?

Evidently not. She got to her feet, folded the twenty, found the wallet in her purse under a pile of fetid clothing. She put the bill in the wallet, yawned, drank more Cutty Sark, stretched, scratched her itching pubic hair, yawned again, and fell heavily onto the bed.

The apartment was on Fifteenth Street near Eighth. The landlord called it an apartment, anyway. She called it a room with a toilet. It had four walls and a window that faced on another window. The people across the courtyard had a good thing going, she thought. She had never been particularly modest, and she kept forgetting to draw the window-shade when she got a man there. What the hell—let the Spics get a good eyeful. Let 'em get all hot and have more babies. Swell the relief rolls, men. Let's have a few more little brats on welfare.

The next drink killed the bottle. She walked to the window and looked across the courtyard. There was a Puerto Rican girl standing at the opposite window, eyes wide, staring at Vicki's body.

"Diddle yourself!" she called. But maybe the little slut didn't understand English. She shrugged, held out one hand with her middle finger extended in a universal gesture. The Puerto Rican girl gaped and fled from the window.

Vicki leaned out the window so that her full breasts brushed against the sill and dropped the empty Cutty Sark bottle, then stood listening for the crash. She was on the third floor and she didn't have to wait very long. When the bottle shattered she grinned briefly and turned away from the window.

Another dead soldier gone to hell, she thought. A mate for the sailor, anyway, who was dead from the neck up at least. And from the navel down, after the workout she'd given him. He'd been a lot of fun, whatever the hell his name was. Allie Casino? Toro Molina? Santa Lucia?

To hell with him, name and all. He'd been kicks, but he was evidently not a hell of a lot brighter than the guy who had left her the twenty, and equally inadequate when it came to diagnosing nymphomania and prescribing the right treatment for the affliction. If he'd had a brain in his head he wouldn't have left her there, not for as long as he had. He'd have stayed right there, next to her, and he'd have been damn sure to be around when she woke up.

Because she woke up hot and bothered as a general rule. And when she woke up she wanted a man around. If the simple seaman thought she was going to cool her heels among other things until he came galumphing back, he had rocks in his head. When you have an itch, you scratch it. If it's in a place you can't reach all by yourself, you find someone to scratch it for you. And you do this in a hurry because an unattended itch can drive a girl out of her mind, among other things.

She tossed herself back down on the bed, lying on her back, her hands folded on her belly like a corpse in a casket. Her skin was gritty, smelly. The sailor had been no bed of roses, of course. And the other guy—doctor? lawyer? Indian chief?—had worked up a sweat of his own. Spend enough time with enough men and you wound up stinking like a whorehouse on a Sunday morning. The hell with it, she thought. She didn't feel like taking a shower. And she didn't mind smelling like a sex factory either. It was a good, healthy smell. She didn't mind it at all.

She looked at her hands. Dead hands, she thought. Well, it shouldn't really take that much longer. She was twenty-eight. The way she drank and the way she fornicated, either her liver or her insides ought to give out within the next five years. Then they could fold her hands over her belly and put her in a box and drop the box into a hole. And shovel dirt on the lid, and put up a little marker. With what inscription?

Here Lays Vicki Flagg
As Usual

That wouldn't be bad. Maybe they would bury her naked; she could make that her last request. Naked, in a deep casket so that they could pose her with her knees up and her thighs parted, in death as in life.

She sighed, scratched herself, then ran her smelly hands over her smelly body. She cupped her smelly breasts and gave them a quick squeeze. Still firm, she noted with approval. It was amazing; a good pair of boobs could take one hell of a pounding without losing their shape. With luck they would outlast her liver and she could wear them to the grave.

She tweaked her nipples, playfully, and then something happened. Goddamn she thought. Here we go again. It never failed.

She hadn't even had to do that during the afternoon. She had come awake all at once—she never woke up slowly, always just opened her eyes at daylight or nightlight and reached for the bottle the sailor had bought. Before she finished chugging it she was hotter than the boiler room in Hell. Get up, get dressed and get out. Then find a man in a bar, walk right up to him and unzip his fly before he knows where the hell he is.

They took a cab to her apartment—no, just call it a furnished room with a toilet. She had him for the first time right there in the cab, with the driver watching in fascination through the rearview mirror. She had him with her skirt bunched around her waist and her feet hanging foolishly out of the cab's open window. She almost asked the cabby afterward if he wanted to try his luck, but the guy in the back seat had plenty of steam of his own and she dragged him up to her room for more of the same.

And now, natch, she wanted it again.

She showered, anyway. The bathroom was in the hall and the shower spray was alternately too hot and too cold, but she took a quick shower and washed the layer of scum from her skin. Just before she left the tub she did something cute with the big bar of soap. It tickled, and set her off worse than ever . . .

Back to her room. Sweater on—no bra, who needs it? Skirt

on—no panties, who needs them? Shoes on—no stockings, no socks, who etc. Purse in hand, out the door, down the stairs, onto the street, away we go.

She went into a bar on Eighth Avenue and broke the twenty on a triple shot of Scotch. The twenty was a good dividend, after all. She only had sixteen bucks left plus change, and the alimony check wasn't due for a few days. It would be on time. It always was. But sixteen bucks was hard to stretch over three or four days even with some man paying for most of the liquor. Thirty-six was a little more like it.

She drank the Scotch, ordered another. The barman brought it and set it in front of her. She looked at it for a minute, shrugged, let it stand. She had a fire going under her skirt and she wasn't going to be able to douse it with Scotch. She needed a man for that.

There were two men in the bar. One of them was the bartender. He was old and fat, looked incapable of doing anything about it. Even if he could he wouldn't be able to give her enough to do much good. He might even have a heart attack and die on her. That had damn near happened once, when she'd drained a fat slob dry in a Broadway hotel. He collapsed on her, and for a horrible minute or two she thought he was dead. She looked at him and saw him stark naked with his hands folded on his fat gut, she got so scared and sick and nervous that she staggered out of the bed and threw up in the middle of the floor. Vicki Flagg, sex killer. Murder the hard way.

But then he stirred, rolled over, winked at her, beckoned to her. Ready for more? Not her, not now, thanks but no thanks. We'll take a rain check, sweetness.

No rain check now. The bartender wouldn't do, no doubt

couldn't do, and the other man had a girl with him. It was something of a shame, because the other man would have been worth a tumble. He was dark and looked vaguely sinister. He was wearing a lamp-black suit and short-brimmed hat, and he looked like George Raft playing Lucky Luciano.

I'll bet he's a stallion, she thought. I'll bet he can go all night without sweating. I'll bet he knows four ways I don't even know about. I'll bet—

Cancel all bets, she told herself. It's a moot point, Vicki kid. Somebody's already got him.

Somebody was a pint-sized blonde with a button nose and skin-tight red dress. Whore Row Goes To the Movies, she thought bitterly. If the old stallion had to have a hooker, why couldn't he settle for her? She was just as much of a tramp as the baby blonde and there was more of her.

She threw the Scotch down her throat and waited for it to hit bottom. She rubbed her thighs together, felt the heat building up inside her. Hurry, she thought. Get to another bar and get another man, for God's sake. Hurry.

Too late.

She didn't do it voluntarily. It just happened, the way things always seemed to happen to Vicki. One moment she was sitting on a bar stool, pressing a shot glass down on the top of the bar and trying to stop shaking like a windblown aspen. The next moment she was sitting on a bar stool at the other end of the bar next to Mr. Syndicate. She was pressing her breasts against the side of his arm, squeezing his thigh with one hand, running the fingers of the other hand through his oily hair, nuzzling her hot wet mouth to his ear, his throat, kissing him and making the sounds of a bitch in heat.

"Come on," she moaned. "Let's go, let's get out of here, come on, let's go—"

Inside, she was dying. Wrong, she was telling herself. Wrong, wrong, wrong. Not exactly subtle, Vicki-O, not subtle at all. Wrong from beginning to end. Vixen Vickie, you have played your cards poorly. You'd better fold, Vick. You've got a bad hand.

The man pulled away, staring at her, holding a hand up in front of himself as if for protection.

"Hey," he was saying. "What the hell are you trying to prove, kid?"

"I want you."

Someone else must have said that, she thought. Not her. She wasn't that stupid.

"If this is some kind of a con—"

"It isn't."

He was looking at her now, his eyes embracing her body. He reached out a hand, held her breast. She couldn't stand it now. The breast felt as though it was on fire. Any moment, she thought, and it'll start smoldering.

He squeezed her breast.

He was very strong and he didn't hold anything back. The pain was razor-sharp, hellfire hot, and she very nearly screamed. She tried to scream, as a matter of fact, but the scream never had a chance. Halfway home it turned into a moan that was animal hunger set to music.

"No con," he said, tonelessly. "If it was a con that would have hurt you, kid. But you loved it."

She couldn't keep her hands off him. She started nuzzling him again, hands groping for him. The blonde was looking switchblades at her and it didn't matter. Nothing mattered, nothing but getting out of the bar and out of the sweater and into a bed or an alleyway or a gutter or anything. Nothing else made the slightest difference in the world.

"This," he said, "I cannot pass up."

"Come on—"

But the blonde started to bitch. "Dan, you came with me. Dan, you're with me tonight. Dan, you don't need this tramp, she's some kind of a whore, you're with me, Dan, Danny, Dan, you're with me—"

A goddamn broken record.

Dan slapped the blonde. He did this very deliberately, drawing back one hand and giving her the back of it across the face. The blonde fell back crying. The bartender remained diplomatically silent. Dan slapped the baby blonde again and she stumbled off the bar stool and almost fell on her face.

He said: "There's enough to go around."

"Dan—"

"I got plenty," he said. "This should be fun. Two broads in a bed. This should be a lot of fun, kid. Both of you kids, this should be fun."

He pushed Vicki aside, got to his feet, reached for a bill and dropped it on top of the bar. He grabbed hold of the blonde with one hand and reached for Vicki with the other. She dodged him momentarily, grabbed the glass he had abandoned and drained it in a single swallow. It tasted like a rum coke but she didn't have time to worry what it was. He had hold of her now, his hand tight on her upper arm, and he was half-leading and half-dragging her toward the door.

The blonde said: "I don't want to share you, Dan. I want you all to myself."

"Not tonight, kid. I would kill you."

"What do you mean?"

"This broad got to me," he said. "Kid, if you tried to take care of me by yourself I would wear you out. I would kill you, kid. I need more than you got."

"You know what I got, Dan!"

"I know," he said. "I have been there before. It is nice."

"Damn right it's nice."

"But," he said. "But it is not enough. Not tonight, kid." He turned to Vicki. "You got a name, kid?"

"Vicki Flagg."

"I am Dan," he said. "The kid here is Judy. That there is my car. Come on, kid. Get your hands away from there, kid. You got the hottest pants I ever saw in my life. One of these days you will set them on fire and burn up the best thing you got, you know that? I think we better use it up before you burn it up, kid."

The car was a black Lincoln. Dan got behind the wheel and the blonde managed to dive into the spot next to him. Vicki got the window, which was not exactly the way she had wanted it. If she was sitting next to him, they would never get to wherever the hell they were supposed to be going. Sooner or later he'd stop for a traffic light, and when that happened, she'd keep him busy for the next three hours.

Fun, she thought. Just go at it in the middle of the street for a day or two. It would stop traffic, goddammit. But they might get a ticket or something.

But Jeez, she thought, this was going to be one for the books. She had played a lot of games, had gone every route she ever heard of. But she never went for more than one person at a time. Line-ups, yes. Midnight reviews, also yes. Gang bangs, call them whatever you wanted. Once in Yorkville she had gone down for fifteen kids in a cellar club, one after the other, climaxing the evening with a stud named Tony who practically bit her breasts off.

But three in a bed? That was a new stunt. And sharing a guy with another girl was a new stunt too. It was going to be a wingding, by God. She only hoped he had a lot of liquor around, because she was going to need it.

Scotch, bourbon, wood alcohol—it didn't matter much. When you were a lush you drank anything alcoholic. And if you were a nympho you went down anywhere and for anybody in the world.

But she hoped he'd have plenty of liquor.

He had plenty of liquor. He also had a penthouse apartment on East Fifty-Third Street. He had, in addition, more money than Aristotle Onassis, as far as she could tell.

A gangster, she thought. A rich gangster—that was the best kind, of course. A rich gangster who would last all night without giving up the ship. A well-endowed gangster who could wear out two broads without working up a sweat.

He didn't want her to drink.

"Kid," he said, "you'll need all your energy. You will not want to be stoned out of your head. You should lay off the sauce, kid, because a drunk broad is not a good broad, and you got to be a good broad for Dan."

"Don't worry," she said. She poured Scotch into a water tumbler until the tumbler started to overflow. She started to drink it, and in a surprisingly short time the glass was empty.

"Kid," he said, "You will now fall flat on your face, which is a shame."

She didn't. Instead she grabbed for him, wondering why he had to call everybody kid. It made things confusing enough when they were just having a drink or riding in the Lincoln. But it would be even worse when the three of them were in bed together. He would give an order and they wouldn't know which one of them he wanted.

Oh, hell, she thought. We'll just take turns and he won't have to say a word.

Dan took off his jacket, his tie, his shirt. She stood there, looking at him, then looking at the tiny blonde. The blonde was not moving. Dan took off his shoes, his socks, his slacks, his underwear. When she saw him she didn't need any instructions.

She tore off her clothes, ripped the sweater up over her head, kicked her shoes halfway across the room, tore the skirt off and let it lie in a heap on the floor. He reached for her and she fell into his arms, her nails digging at his buttocks, her breasts drilling holes in his chest, her mouth hungry, her tongue darting down his throat.

"Kid," he said. "Peel."

He couldn't mean her. He had to mean the blonde. She went on rubbing against him, snatching at him, kissing him, while the blonde undressed. The blonde was small—no more than five feet tall—but the blonde was not exactly scrawny. Her breasts and buttocks would have looked slightly oversized on a tall girl. On the blonde, they looked enormous.

The blonde moved now. Vicki was pressed face-to-face against Dan, her breasts against his chest, and Judy was coming up behind him, throwing her arms around him from the rear. He was the meat in a sandwich, Vicki thought hysterically. A big hunk of meat between two slices of broad.

"The bed," he said.

She didn't know where the bed was. But she found out, because the three of them went to it. It was in the bedroom, appropriately enough; and it was a big bed, which was fortunate. Three people tend to clutter an ordinary bed. They tend to pile up.

Which they did anyway. They would have piled up in the Sahara Desert, the way they were disporting themselves. And it was getting to be one hell of a scene, a brand new one on Vicki. They were still playing sandwich, with Dan between her and Judy, and she couldn't take much more of this. The preliminaries could drive a girl nuts.

Time for the main event, she thought. Get those bums out of the ring! Bring in the heavyweights!

Then she was lying on her back, knees high. The classic position, she thought. Vicki Flagg's standard pose. And he was telling Judy that it would be her turn next. But Vicki barely heard the words. She was too wrapped up in something else entirely.

Judy didn't go away. Judy was still fulfilling her function as a slice of bread, lying on top of Dan. The bedsprings were wailing symphonically, and the world started to go around.

Faster—

Faster—

Her hands were on Dan's buttocks. Her nails were raking his flesh and drawing blood as he surged again and again into her. And then, on the backs of her hands, she felt the soft fire of Judy.

What the hell, she thought. Let's all have a ball. What the hell.

Then the earth began to go tipsy, topsy and turvy, swinging in six different directions at once. She was holding Dan tightly against her and she was holding Judy. Her breasts ached, her groin ached, she was a sheet of flame from head to toe. The world dipped and dove, and there was thunder and lightning, the hurricane's eye winked, and then, then, then she went off like a fifty-megaton bomb. Boom!

It was one hell of an evening no matter how you looked at it. It wasn't even evening, to be honest. It was morning, two in the morning, and she was sitting on the edge of the bed knocking hell out of a fresh fifth of J&B. In the middle of the bed, more or less, Dan was doing something delicious to Judy. And she wasn't even jealous.

Not at all.

Not in the least.

Not a bit.

She felt too good to be jealous. She had felt good before, now and then, but never this good. She had felt good just the other night at the Dorchester with the sailor—Addie Marino? Dodo Mitcowitz? The hell with his name. But she had not felt nearly this good, because the sailor was not this good.

No one was.

Dan was amazing. She had had him five or six times already, and in-between he had Judy, and some of the times he had both of them at once, a neat trick unless you happen to be a freak. But no matter how you looked at it, she had been resoundingly boffed five or six times. She wasn't sure of the precise count. It was hard to keep track.

She swigged more Scotch. One thing was sure—she wasn't getting drunk. She was drinking like a fish, and she'd already managed to make a dent in Dan's liquor supply. But it was not getting to her. Maybe she was sweating it out before it could get into her blood. Something like that.

More Scotch. She turned again to look at the couple on the bed.

Hey, she thought.

"Hey," she said.

Nobody answered her.

Dan was lying on his back, smiling gently, eyes closed. Judy had a look of dreamy lust on her little-girl face.

"Hurry," she said.

Because it was getting to her, dammit. It was reaching her, there was no getting away from it, she just had to get into the act or she would go crazy.

Slut, she thought. Slut, bitch, tramp—don't you ever ever ever get enough?

Hell, Vicki thought. And double-hell. All right, kiddies. Make room for Vicki. Enough, my friends, is plenty. Enough is more than enough. But I never get enough, so we have to make a threesome out of this.

She looked at Dan's face. His eyes closed, his lips parted slightly, curved in a smile. She looked for several seconds at his face.

Then she sat on it . . .

Chapter 10

The trouble was: Nothing ever seemed real. Judy Warren sat in her white negligee on the fluffy white chair in her white-walled living room watching the white phone on the black table. It was like a scene in a movie, as always. She didn't feel like Judy Warren waiting for a gangster named Dan Starke to call and apologize. She felt like June Allyson waiting for Peter Lawford to ring up and sing "I'm Sorry" after their musical misunderstanding in the last scene.

Life had been like that to her as long as she could remember. It was the result of seeing too many movies and reading too many screen magazines when she was a kid. Somewhere along the star-dusted path she had left reality; life had become just a succession of celluloid scenes, some with songs, some with melodramatic dialogue, some with just tragic moody music (usually conducted by Percy Faith) in the background. She was Vera Ellen and Dan was twinkle-toed Donald O'Connor two-stepping her off her feet. Or she was a lusty Lana Turner (and he was a cruelly-smiling Clark Gable) fainting in his strong arms. Or she might be a sultry sophisticated Debora Kerr and Dan was an enchanting, sophisticated Cary Grant who would grip her gently by the shoulders and murmur "By-bee, yew don't know what yew *do* to me."

Even when they were in the act of love, she never felt it as much as saw it projected on a screen inside her eyelids. They would be sinking slowly to the couch, below the window level—before the camera level. She would only see the landscape outside the window as the camera panned up, and the whispers would come to her quietly, although in stereophonic sound. There would be the delicious ruffling of silken petticoats as Mantovani led five hundred violent violins in a soaring crescendo of throbbing melody. Then the midnight sky would explode in multi-color fireworks (because she was Ginger Rogers and he was William Holden and it was Mardi Gras time in New Orleans); her heart was filled with the blossoming reds and streaking blues and flaming yellows, until a veritable garden of blooming explosions by Technicolor DeLuxe filled her Cinemascope mind, and they reached their ecstatic heights together—she and Dan and Ginger and William and Mantovani!

Except it was hard to imagine last night's performance on a theater screen. First of all she was faced with a big casting problem for the part of that nymph slut, Vicki. Secondly, she had not heard any music then—only their own groans and the sounds of their grinding bodies. Third, what the three of them had done together would not have been permitted to be shown even in Hoboken. If filmable at all, their little physical triangle was strictly an Italian import. She didn't like those at all because they were always too raunchy and usually ended unhappily.

She crossed her legs, jiggled her foot and watched the white phone, waiting.

Why didn't it ring? Why doesn't he call and apologize? June Allyson never had to wait this long. Twenty or thirty seconds at the most, then the phone would jingle. She would look relieved, and then uncertain. She would face the camera, the phone would ring again and everybody in the audience would be urging her to pick it up. But she wouldn't because she was fighting a great private battle between love and pride. The phone would ring a third time and then the camera would show Peter, looking distraught and anguished in a booth at Grand Central, communicating by his complex expression that he would let it ring once more and then take that train back to Slocum Falls alone and forget her forever.

Back to June. The phone rings that last time. She reaches for it, draws back, hesitates, reaches for it again and snatches it to her ear. The music begins.

June: "Hello?"

Peter: "June?"

June: "Peter?"

Peter: "Yes, darling. Oh darling, I'm so sorry—"

June: (giddy with happiness) "Oh it's all right, darling. You called, you called. That's all that matters. Oh Peter, I love you."

Dan Starke, you louse, Judy thought. I hate your rotten guts. She stared at the phone hostilely.

All right, you lousy SOB, go ahead and play bedroom bowling with that sex-crazy tramp. If all you want is someone to lay, you're damn right she can outlast me. She can outlast you too, Mr. Second-Class Capone. She'll use you 'til you can't stand up, then she'll twitch her butt and walk out on you. Then where the hell will you be? Come back to me, Mr. Tough-Talk? Shove that up your pinball machine! I'm not going to even be here when you finally get around to calling.

She stood up, flounced into her bedroom and began to get dressed.

It wasn't right at all. It was all goddamn wrong. It never happened like this in the movies. But then—face it, Judy, old kid—this wasn't the movies. You weren't June Allyson, with a face like a vanilla malter; and he sure as hell wasn't any Peter Lawford. You were just plain old Judy Warren. No, not even that. That was another little bit of playacting. You were Judy Warzynski from Conestoga, Pennsylvania, home of the famous Conestoga wagon (whatever the hell that was) and not much more. You were just a twenty-three year old stage-struck little sleep-around with no talent, no voice, no ability beyond that of holding up a pair of mammaries that were three sizes too big for you.

She paused, putting on her bra and inspected her talent in the mirror. What she could do, she did well. There was a little bit of a sag but when you were only five feet, one quarter inch tall and had thirty-eight C's in your holster, something had to give a little here or there. They were plenty good bazooms, though, all said and done. And just about everything had been said about them and done to them. They had been patted by her high school English teacher and stroked by six slobbering boy friends and squeezed by that phony buzzard who was going to make her Miss Conestoga Wagon of 1959. Those ruby nipples had been tweaked by the agent who booked her in the chorus line of the Naughty-Naughty Club, pulled by the club's pianist. Finally they had been kissed and nuzzled and suckled by none other than the notorious kingpin of the juke box and pinball rackets—a man who could hold out his hairy palm and say, "See that, kid? That is all of Brooklyn I am holding right there."

The hell with all of Brooklyn, Mr. Daniel Starowski Starke. Drop the whole stinking borough into one of your juke box slots and see if it'll make love to you. Because I sure as hell won't anymore.

She put her hands under her breasts and squeezed them, the nipples pointing straight at the mirror image. Rat-tat-tat-tat-tat-tat, she thought, swiveling her torso to gun down everything within the width of the mirror. She turned, tossed her can defiantly and got dressed.

It was four in the afternoon and she was prancing down Fifth Avenue in a tight red jersey dress with her silver fox swishing about her shoulders. She had walked six blocks—from 65th to 59th—looked at thirty-eight store windows, entered four stores and made a total of eleven purchases which totaled seven hundred and fifty-three dollars. And twelve cents. All on Dan Starke's account.

And she wasn't nearly finished either. If he was going to kiss her off, it was going to cost him a pretty little penny. He could have his lousy little apartment back, but he'd have to kill her before he'd get the clothes and jewelry from her. And she was going to pick up a few more vital items before he got around to crossing her name off his accounts.

At Fifty-Ninth, she entered Bergdorf Goodman, took the elevator up to the fifth floor and gave the saleswoman a nice commission on a white *Peau d'Ange* ball gown. Only $160. Hell, she had never been to a ball in her life, but it would be nice to have. Maybe she'd just wear it for balling—some other guy.

Down another block and into Tailored Woman, fourth floor, coat salon. There were two mink collared coats she liked. One was a sleek worsted faille, black with pastel mink; the other way grey with taupe mink. Both, the pristine salesgirl informed her, were "extraordinarily priced at only $139.95 each." Cheap, she thought. A real bargain. Hell, she'd show Dan what a budget-buyer she was. "I'll take them both," she told the girl.

"They look lovely on petite women," the girl said, sealing the deal.

Judy smiled. Petite your behind, she thought.

Outside again, with a vicious little grin on her face. How much did that make now? A little over a grand. Well, she'd get Dan a present too, just to show that she was always thinking about him. At Forty-eighth she went into Black Starr & Gorham—"Creators of Beautiful Jewels for Over 150 Years," a dignified little sign said.

She looked at a dozen pins before she found the one that she liked. It was a hand-sculptured unicorn with a big horn and a bejeweled collar. Eighteen carat gold, of course. A steal at two and a half if you liked emeralds, rubies or sapphires in the collar. An absolute give-away at two eighty-five with diamonds.

She picked the diamonds, of course.

"The name, please?" the Reginald Gardner character behind the counter inquired.

"The account is Daniel Starke. My name is Judy Warren."

"Of course, Miss Warren. I should have remembered. I had the pleasure of serving you and Mr. Starke on one other occasion. If you'll just sign here, please."

She signed with a flourish.

"Do you wish to take the pin with you or have it delivered?"

"Delivered, please."

"Certainly. The name and address?"

"Mr. Daniel Starke." She smiled as she dictated the address. She really should put in a little card. 'Here's a little unicorn. If you don't like it, why don't you let your nymph try it on for size?'

No, no card. She wouldn't waste the time on him.

Out on Fifth again and into the Fifth Avenue for a bite to eat. Just a petite little late lunch with all the other after-matinee matrons. A shrimp salad and a daiquiri. Two daiquiris. She liked the way they made them. And a nice tip for the waitress who looked like Ann Sheridan.

And now what? It was almost five and the streets were beginning to glut up with the working classes, the snub-faced snub-breasted career women hurrying to get home, get plastered, get naked and call up some beefy stevedore; the young high-seamed, high-skirted secretaries who, if they didn't have a date to play "Button, button, here comes my roommate" with would have to curl up with a dirty best seller; the hat-box swinging models with their carefully coiffed hair and shaved wazoos—so that the suckers couldn't see anything too intimate when they turned the lingerie ads upside down. Well, she wasn't going to stand around and get bumped by all those hard frontal works and basketball behinds. So—

Into a movie, of course.

One of the cheap theaters on Forty-Second was showing an old double feature she couldn't resist. *Duel in the Sun* with Gregory Peck, Joseph Cotton, Jennifer Jones and a thousand others. Also: *Treasure of Sierra Madre,* Humphrey Bogart. Jeez, how she loved Bogie. He was real tough, not like some other imitation hoodlum whom she could name.

She walked in near the end of *Duel in the Sun.* Gregory and

Jennifer were both almost dead and she was crawling up a great big goddamn mountain to get to him for one final scene before they kicked off in each other's arms. The sun was burning down and it didn't look like old Jennie would make it. But of course she would. Hell, she had seen this one three times before. She didn't even have to watch the screen to know what was happening. The music was all straining and struggling and sweating and blood.

She closed her eyes and pictured Dan with a few nice holes in his gut hanging over the edge of the mountain stretching out his hand to her. And here she came, crawling on her stomach, an inch at a time. Impossible. She'd rub her breasts raw. But that didn't matter. He was her man. Up, up, up. Christ that sun was hot and she had a few extra openings in her too. But she crawled on. Only a few feet more now. She heard him moan. The music was dizzying. Only a foot now, inches. She reached out for his hand, grasped it and suddenly it wasn't his hand anymore. It was the thin bony hand of that slut, Vicki, and it began to play with her fingers.

She stood up, on the top of the mountain and there was Dan, not bleeding at all, not looking anything but goddamn happy, naked and working on that grinning nymph.

She opened her eyes. Greg and Jennie were necking their last few seconds away.

Then she felt an arm about her shoulder.

Then she smelled all of Scotland leaning next to her.

"Hey there, honey," the bum rasped. "You're all right, you know that?"

She pushed his hand off, but it came back as if on a string. She started to rise and, then the second man pushed in on her other side. His rough hand went to her leg and scooted up under her dress.

She gave him an elbow in the stomach and dug her nails into the first bum's face. He screamed as the second one started to cough. She stood up, kicking out blindly, got herself an ankle that brought forth another scream from her left and the bracing of the seat in front of her which brought forth her own cry. Then, stamping, she was out in the aisle.

People were standing up all around her, and there came the usher waving her flashlight wildly. She pushed past an ice cream man and found herself another seat five rows down.

But she had lost her interest in the picture. She watched the first half-hour of the Bogie film. But the rising hills of the Sierra Madres began to look like Vicki Flagg's thrusting breasts and she couldn't take it any longer.

Hell, she thought, even Bogie had deserted her. That stinking whore had everyone.

She took a cab—driven by Gregory Ratoff—back to her apartment, made herself a stiff drink, sat down on the fluffy white chair and waited.

This time she did not have to wait long. In twenty minutes the phone rang. She jumped, reached for it, then drew back. June Allyson, she thought. Play it cool.

The phone rang again and this time she grabbed it up. She'd say Hello and then Peter would say June? and then Darling.

"Hello," she said.

"Hi, kid," said Dan Starke's insufferably cocky voice.

"What do you want?"

"That is not an easy question to answer, kid. I want a great many different things."

"Your friend leave yet or you just taking a coffee break?"

He laughed. "She has vacated my premises for the duration."

"That's what I thought. Well I'm vacating your premises over here as soon as I can get my things packed."

"Kid—"

"Nuts to you, Mr. Big Shot."

"Now, kid. Is that any way to talk to the best friend you will ever have? Is it not true that Dan has treated you fair and square all the way down the line? Is it not also true that perhaps Dan had one drink too many last night which was the reason that he acted a little more liberally than you might expect a man of his position to act?"

"You weren't drunk. You wanted that slut. More than you wanted me."

"Leave us say that my affections were equally divided at the time. If you had not made such a hasty departure I am certain you would have received more than your full share of Dan's attentions."

"You were kissing her like you said you'd never kiss any broad but me."

"All that as it may be. If you recall the exact circumstances, there was very little I had to say about that."

"Well, you can just get yourself another girl. We're finished."

"Kid, you are talking in anger which you will regret in the morning. Dan will be generous and forgive this little outburst. I will call again tomorrow when clearer heads prevail."

"Well, you won't find me here, Mr. Juke-Box. I can promise you that."

"Kid—"

The crash of the receiver on the cradle cut the sentence. She stood there for a moment, fuming. Then she crossed to the table, finished her drink. She poured herself another straight shot, finished that, then poured herself another and sat down.

The phone rang. She looked at it but didn't move.

It rang again. Ring your tail off, she thought.

The phone rang its tail off. And then it stopped.

Good, she thought. Now get on your goddamn train to Slocum Falls and leave me alone.

But she knew she didn't mean it. If he called again, she'd talk to him and let him smooth her with a little present of say, a diamond bracelet that would set him back a couple of grand.

She waited, sipping her drink, watching the phone. It didn't ring again.

All right. So he probably went out looking for that whore again, or somebody else. Well if he could find outside interests, so could she. If they decided to get back together again later, fine. But she would have tried out somebody else first. They'd start even. Right now she was going to get her oven stoked.

She found her stoker an hour later. It took her forty-five minutes to shower and change into a black sweater that could not have fitted her when she was twelve, a tight blue skirt, tinted stockings and the highest pair of heels she owned. She brushed her hair out and let it hang loose, slipped into a raincoat, snatched up a black purse on strings and lit a cigarette. She knew how she looked and it was just the way she wanted to look: Marlene Dietrich waiting under a street lamp for a pick-up.

She smoked her cigarette down waiting for the elevator, lit a new one in the lobby, waved off the doorman who had his whistle in mouth ready to signal for a cab. That accounted for ten minutes more.

It took her five more—rounding out the hour—before the man came up to her at the corner. She had a cigarette burning so he could not open up with the time-honored line of offering her a light. He settled for a boy-meets-girl gambit of: "Hi. Waiting for me?"

She looked him over once before she answered. He was tall, dark-haired, dressed in collegiate-turned-executive style, a friendly smile and a nose that was just a trifle oversized. An old Tony Perkins or a young Raymond Massey, she thought.

"Sure," she said. "Let's go." She would have liked to say it in French, or at least with Marlene's French accent. But she knew the way it would sound with her nasal voice. And besides, she didn't know any acceptable French.

They went to the nearest bar. He ordered rye and she had bourbon. They made pass-the-time conversation. No, she wasn't from New York. Yes, he was. They agreed it was a big city. Yes, he worked on Madison Avenue. No, she wasn't a showgirl. Not really, she amended with a smile, although she had worked in a few clubs. Between engagements now, she said.

They had a second round and his hand went under the table and rested on her thigh.

Nice weather for this time of year. Oh very. You live around here? Right up the block, she said. You? Afraid not; like to though—with the same friendly smile. His hand stroked her knee gently, tentatively.

They smoked, they smiled at each other, the waitress (Thelma Ritter) emptied their ashtray. He ordered another round.

"You don't mind, do you?" "Of course not." "Say, we're getting along fine, aren't we?" "Swell," she said.

On the third round he got around to it. That is to say, his hand was under her dress kneading the soft flesh of her inner thigh. Then, as an afterthought: "Why don't we get out of here and go someplace where we can be alone?"

"Fine," she said. About time, she thought.

They got up. He left a dollar for Thelma Ritter and paid the bartender, played by William Bendix, for their drinks.

Arms around each other's waists, they strolled down the street.

"I'm afraid my place isn't much," he said. "Just a room in a cheap hotel uptown."

What would Marlene say then, she wondered. Come to mine? No, Marlene would live in a cellar even rattier than his place. Recast then. She was Rita Hayworth in her elegant little penthouse. No, try again. Zsa-Zsa Gabor? A little better.

"We could go to my little room, dollink," she said.

He laughed at the imitation not the suggestion. He scratched his head. "Wal—uh—now."

Jimmy Stewart, she thought.

"Well, why not?" He finally finished, and winked.

Not quite Errol Flynn but it would do.

The doorman, looking like Sidney Poitier, grinned whitely as he bowed them inside. He lit her cigarette as they waited for the car and they rode up in silence. In the light, she gave him a second once-over.

Not bad, she concluded. A little rough around the tweed elbows but all in all, not bad.

Once inside, she let him help her off with her coat and then moved to the small bar.

"Let me," he said.

Dashing, she thought. Doug Fairbanks.

He joined her on the couch as they drank. His hand went to her shoulder, to her neck, tilted her chin up. She smiled; they kissed and Mantovani and his boys came up with "Love in Bloom."

They held the kiss through an encore and into "My Foolish Heart," where his hand finally touched. He rubbed over the tip of one breast easily. She moaned. He rubbed the other. She lay back.

No faking, she thought. No protests. No Margaret O'Brien stuff. She let his arms go around her, their mouths mesh, their tongues touch. She squirmed and pressed her knee against his thigh.

He got the idea and smiled as if it were his own. His hand slid up her leg and under her dress, not stopping at the thigh this time.

The symphony began, "Love Is A Many Splendored Thing" and she decided to get on with it. She toyed with a button on his shirt. Cute. Tuesday Weld-ish.

He let her open three buttons before he decided to get into the act. Smiling, his hand slipped under her sweater and tried to reach the clasp of her bra. No dice. He'd have to be plastic man to get at it from that position.

She stood up and gave him that mature-woman-taking-young-man-in-hand look. Simone Signoret in *Room At The Top.* An Academy Award performance.

And in record time, the sweater came up and off, the bra unsnapped and fell, the skirt unzippered and dropped, followed by the stockings and then—Ladies and Gentlemen, the winner is—the panties went. She stood before him naked and glowing.

She waited while he undressed and then led him to the bedroom.

Nude as babes and hand in hand they crawled onto her bed, threw their arms about each other, locked their mouths together. Up Music. "I've Never Felt Like This Before!"

Garbo and Gable—Together Again and Better than Ever.

Well, almost.

His arms tightened about her and she went limp, letting the waves of passion wash over her, warm and gentle, building, soothing. He was Burt Lancaster, she thought, seeing the breakers crash against the rocks and lick over them in long wet tongues.

The music swelled, encompassing them. And here came the fireworks, and more waves, and stallions smashing their hooves on stable walls, and drummers beating out a wild tattoo.

It was dizzying, the Cinerama roller-coaster. It was deeper 3-D. She felt herself expanding all the way. Vista Vision!

And then with the thundering of Ben Hur's chariots in the background she turned and squirmed and pulled at him, reveling in the thought: Around The World In Eighty Days!

The door opened and Broderick Crawford, played by Dan Starke, was standing there.

She screamed and Tony Perkins turned.

"Take care of him," Dan said to his friend, Jack Palance.

She watched, horrified as the bodyguard pulled the man up by the shoulders and clubbed him across the forehead with his gun butt. The man collapsed in a swoon.

"I am not a difficult person," Dan said quietly. "I do not mind if a broad of mine does not want to see me for a while. But I do mind if she is laying for some other guy on the side."

Judy looked at him wide-eyed.

"We will discuss this further as soon as you have put some clothes on," Dan said. "You will start to do that now."

Judy got up and went to the closet.

"In the meantime," Dan said, "we will get on with the business of disposing of your former friend here. Artie, will you please get me this person's wallet. I like to know whom I am about to have bumped off."

The bodyguard went to the living room and returned in seconds. He handed Dan a wallet.

"This person's name is Miles Carter," Dan said. "I do not believe I have ever made his acquaintance. That is all to the better. I do not like to do away with anyone who is within my circle of friends. Artie, dispose of Miles Carter now."

Artie took a silencer out of his pocket, attached it to his pistol, put the gun to Miles Carter's head and pulled the trigger. The sound was the popping of a champagne cork.

"Thank you," Dan said. "Now Judy, you and I will depart from these premises while Artie takes care of the unpleasant details of removing Miles Carter's body."

Judy dressed hurriedly, trembling. When she had finished she came and stood before Dan.

"You look very nice," he said with a smile. "Dan likes to see his broads look nice." He put his arm around her waist. "Dan is a very generous man. His heart is as big as all outdoors. All is forgiven." He grinned. "Come, leave us depart this place."

Hand in hand, they walked to the door. Dan opened it just as Artie was dragging Miles Carter's body into the living room.

"It is unfortunate about Miles Carter," Dan said. "But also I think that it is just as well. Although I have never met the person previously, I have the feeling that he is the kind who could start a lot of trouble." He shrugged. "But then I have been wrong before. Leave us go."

They went.

My Newsletter: I get out an email newsletter at unpredictable intervals, but rarely more often than every other week. I'll be happy to add you to the distribution list. A blank email to lawbloc@gmail.com with "newsletter" in the subject line will get you on the list, and a click of the "Unsubscribe" link will get you off it, should you ultimately decide you're happier without it.

Lawrence Block has been writing award-winning mystery and suspense fiction for half a century. You can read his thoughts about crime fiction and crime writers in *The Crime of Our Lives,* where this MWA Grand Master tells it straight. His most recent novels are *The Girl With the Deep Blue Eyes*; *The Burglar Who Counted the Spoons,* featuring Bernie Rhodenbarr; *Hit Me,* featuring Keller; and *A Drop of the Hard Stuff,* featuring Matthew Scudder, played by Liam Neeson in the film *A Walk Among the Tombstones.* Several of his other books have been filmed, although not terribly well. He's well known for his books for writers, including the classic *Telling Lies for Fun & Profit,* and *The Liar's Bible.* In addition to prose works, he has written episodic television (*Tilt!*) and the Wong Kar-wai film, *My Blueberry Nights.* He is a modest and humble fellow, although you would never guess as much from this biographical note.

Email: lawbloc@gmail.com
Twitter: @LawrenceBlock
Facebook: lawrence.block
Website: lawrenceblock.com

Lightning Source UK Ltd.
Milton Keynes UK
UKHW020955250122
397664UK00009B/2377